"I want to make sure you're okay. That was a nasty bump to the head."

"I'm fine." Bri tugged her hand away, shocked at the way her body keeled toward him. The way her insides melted into liquid at his touch.

Fraser Moore was not good for her resolve. But he was very good for her libido.

"Wait—" He reached out to double-check the cut on her head. Or so she thought. But he paused, fingertips on her temple, then they trailed down to her mouth. His thumb smudged across her lips, making her breath come fast and hard. Thoughts fueled by pure desire swirled in her head. *Touch. Mouth. Taste. Kiss.*

He came closer. His breath warm on the side of her face. For a moment she thought he was going to kiss her. Wanted him to. Ached for that soft pressure of his lips on hers. His head tipped and he tilted her chin up, looking at her with such heat it made her tremble.

Dear Reader,

Many thanks for picking up *Nurse's One-Night Baby Surprise*.

I've indulged myself with yet another trip to the stunning English Lake District for this book… I can't seem to keep away. It's such a wonderfully romantic setting. Unfortunately for our hero, Fraser, his daughter isn't quite so enamored with the place, but he hopes she will fall in love with it and also reconnect with her godmother, Briana Barclay, who lives there, too. What Fraser doesn't bank on is falling for Briana himself!

Briana has many reasons not to trust Fraser, but when he reaches out for help with his tearaway teenager, she reluctantly falls a little under his spell. Neither of them wants a relationship, so they fight hard against the spark of attraction, but when they are forced to work together and socialize together, things get a little…involved!

I loved writing this book and watching the changing dynamics between these two!

I love hearing from readers, so please get in touch via my website, louisageorge.com, or on Facebook, louisageorgebooks.

Happy reading!

Louisa x

NURSE'S ONE-NIGHT
BABY SURPRISE

LOUISA GEORGE

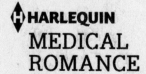

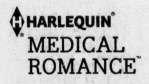

HARLEQUIN®
MEDICAL
ROMANCE™

Recycling programs
for this product may
not exist in your area.

ISBN-13: 978-1-335-40450-3

Nurse's One-Night Baby Surprise

Copyright © 2021 by Louisa George

This edition published by arrangement with Harlequin Books S.A.

For questions and comments about the quality of this book, please contact us at CustomerService@Harlequin.com.

Harlequin Enterprises ULC
22 Adelaide St. West, 40th Floor
Toronto, Ontario M5H 4E3, Canada
www.Harlequin.com

Printed in U.S.A.

Award-winning author **Louisa George** has been an avid reader her whole life. In between chapters she's managed to train as a nurse, marry her doctor hero and have two sons. Now she writes chapters of her own in the medical romance, contemporary romance and women's fiction genres. Louisa's books have variously been nominated for the coveted RITA® Award and the New Zealand Koru Award and have been translated into twelve languages. She lives in Auckland, New Zealand.

Books by Louisa George

Harlequin Medical Romance

Royal Christmas at Seattle General
The Princess's Christmas Baby

SOS Docs
Saved by Their One-Night Baby

The Ultimate Christmas Gift
The Nurse's Special Delivery

The Hollywood Hills Clinic
Tempted by Hollywood's Top Doc

The Last Doctor She Should Ever Date
Tempted by Her Italian Surgeon
Reunited by Their Secret Son
A Nurse to Heal His Heart
A Puppy and a Christmas Proposal

Visit the Author Profile page
at Harlequin.com for more titles.

CHAPTER ONE

'PLEASE, DON'T MAKE me go to school. *Please.*' Fraser blinked fast at the woman in the passenger seat next to him as she stared out at the white-washed stone buildings with their grey-blue slate roofs and the sign 'Welcome to Bowness High School'. 'I've got a tummy ache.' He moaned and rubbed his belly, looking for sympathy.

But she clearly wasn't doling any out today. She frowned, rolled her heavily mascaraed eyes and pulled her ponytail tight. 'No, you haven't. You're fine.'

'Please, don't make me go. Please, Lily.' He tugged on her arm and made sad eyes at her. 'Can you write me a sick note?'

She glared at him. 'Isn't that supposed to be *your* job?'

'I need a responsible person to do it for me,' he teased. 'Know any?'

'Stop it, Dad.' A reluctant smile finally... *finally* curved her lips and she play-punched his arm. 'Honestly, you're worse than me. You have to go. It's work. You've signed a contract and everything. Stop messing about.'

'Made you smile, though.' That would be enough to see him through what he knew were going to be difficult days ahead. Just as the last few months...years, really, had been.

She threw him a look that would have frozen hell. 'Only out of pity.'

'You used to laugh at my jokes.'

'Back when they were funny. Like, when I was six or something.'

Now she was fifteen going on twenty-five. Wearing non-regulation mascara and lip gloss that he'd refused to fight about this morning and a skirt that he was sure hadn't been so short when they'd bought it a couple of weeks ago. He'd decided to let it go for today. *Pick your battles.* First day, new term, new school.

New start.

He remembered her first smile, her first tooth, her first day at nursery as if it were all yesterday. Where had that time gone? How had he ended up with this stroppy, beautiful, fierce teenager when only minutes ago she had been a tiny scrap that had fitted into the crook of his arm?

They'd always been a team and he'd always made her laugh. She'd loved his jokes almost as much as he loved her, but now she blamed him for everything that made her unhappy. He met her eyes—so dark like her mother's—and saw the pain there. And the fear too. He had to make sure she was going to be okay. *That* was his job.

Until five years ago he'd shared that job with his ex. They'd co-parented as best they could with shared custody, living just streets apart, short-term lovers who'd become long-term friends. He'd been the bad cop to Ellen's good cop. Funny, sweet, warm-hearted Ellen who had died, leaving both him and Lily bereft and him to parent on his own, clumsily navigating first their daughter's deep grief and then teenage hormones. And now, in his daughter's eyes, he was just all round bad.

He patted her hand. 'Seriously, Lily, are you okay with this?'

She looked out at the sleet melting on contact with the heated windscreen, her smile dissolving into the sulky expression that had been ever-present on her lips since that icy five-hour drive north had brought them here to the Lake District, where her mother had grown up, leaving their London life behind. That expression had remained all through Christmas and New Year, particularly when they'd been to buy the uniform she was wearing now. Lily didn't want to try. She didn't want a new life, she'd been perfectly content with the old one.

And that was why they'd had to move.

She slid her hand from under his and twisted the handles of her expensive new backpack. If he was honest, she looked about as fed up as he'd ever seen her.

'No.' She shrugged. 'I'm not okay about it and you know that already. But here we are anyway. I don't really get a say in it, do I?'

His heart squeezed. If only Ellen were here, she'd know how to do this. But, then, if Ellen were here, he wouldn't have upped sticks and moved away from all Lily knew. Out of desperation he'd thought of this place. Grasping at flimsy straws, he'd also wondered whether Lily's godmother might have moved back here at some point too…cavalry to enlist to help him. Although he wasn't sure she'd want to help after their last meeting five years ago.

Guilt rattled again. Had it been wise to move Lily so far from everything she knew? From the place where she had memories of her mother?

'It's going to be fun, Lily-Bee, if we just try. A fresh start for us both. It's what we need. Trust me.'

Another dark look. This one said, *I did trust you. Once. But now? Not so much.* 'A freezing start, more like. And boring. B-o-oring.'

'Not once you've made friends.'

'Duh. I have friends, Dad. Lots of them. Back in Clapham.'

They hadn't been friends, they'd been…the only word to describe them was *delinquents.* He knew that made him sound a lot older than his thirty-four years. He'd watched helplessly as she'd changed from a happy little girl into a tearaway teenager who had refused to listen, refused to meet him halfway and refused to conform to even the lightest of rules. He'd been at a total loss as to what to do. So much for being the cool outreach doctor who understood teenagers.

But only a few moments ago he'd finally managed to get a smile from her and he wasn't going to spoil it by raking over those old arguments again. 'With your winning personality and the amazing talents you inherited from me, you'll soon make lots more.'

Just one. One nice one. One that isn't into drugs and drinking. One who actually attends school. Please.

He laughed, trying to show her he was joking, about the talents anyway.

She rolled her eyes. 'Yeah, Dad. Whatever.'

'They have an excellent drama programme.'

'I stopped wanting to be an actress in year three.'

'The science programme has won national awards.'

'I don't want to be a scientist either.'

'What do you want, Lily-Bee?'

'Not to be here.' Her nostrils flared and she glared at him. He wasn't sure if it was because he'd called her by her childhood nickname or because she was here in the car, staring at her future…or both.

'You never know, you might change your mind. Give it a chance.'

Give us a chance.

They'd been all out of chances in London. Next stop for her had been the juvenile detention centre. The local police had had his number on speed dial.

Silence.

He dredged up another smile and his cheerful sing-song Dad voice. 'Right, best get going. I'll see you this afternoon and we can drive home together after my clinic's finished.'

Her eyes narrowed. 'I can walk.'

'It's January. The forecast's for snow. It'll be cold and you're not wearing walking clothes.' He held back the criticism as he looked at the short skirt and school shirt open one button too many, unsure how his city girl would fit into the country school. But it was too late now. They were here and he was determined they'd make the best of it. 'Anyway, it'll be a good chance to chat about our first day at school.'

'You're only going to be here for a couple of hours later. I have to put up with it all day. Every day. Until I die of total boredom.'

'Or you could embrace the delights of rural living in a beautiful place.' Behind the school buildings rugged snow-topped mountains provided a breathtaking backdrop. Or would have, if visibility hadn't been impeded by the low-hanging clouds heavy with sleet. He cleared his throat, deepened his voice and threw his arm out as if he was on stage, delivering an important soliloquy. '"I wandered lonely as a cloud…"'

'Stop it, Dad. Maybe you should be the one doing drama, not me.' Another eye-roll, followed by a tut. 'Promise you won't be embarrassing at school? Like, if you see me in the corridor, don't even acknowledge you know me?'

'Is there no end to the ways you can spear my heart?' he said, trying to put a smile in his voice but remembering how everything his mum had said and done had almost killed him with embarrassment when he'd been Lily's age. It didn't mean her words didn't hurt, though. 'Everyone's going to know eventually, Lily. It's a small school. We have the same surnames. It won't take a genius to work out we're related.'

'Please, just let me have a few precious hours where I'm not the "hot" doctor's daughter?'

She made quotation marks with her fingers and pulled an *I can't believe I just said that about my dad* face, and he tried hard not to laugh.

Hot? To a bunch of teenagers? *Great.* No wonder she was embarrassed. 'Okay. You won't know I'm there. I promise, I'll keep a very low profile.'

'Good. See you later, yeah?'

'Absolutely.' He leaned in to ruffle her hair the

way he'd always done, but she was opening the door and swivelling out of her seat, completely oblivious. Out of reach. 'Good luck for your first day, Lily-Bee.'

A bitter laugh came from her throat. 'Believe me, I'm going to need it.'

Me too, he thought. *More than you'll ever know.*

'He hit me first.' The boy pressed an ice pack to his swollen jaw and shivered. He was holding back tears, trying so hard to be the tough guy. 'It was self-defence, miss. Honest.'

'Hey, I wasn't there and I'm not going to judge, Alfie. You don't have to explain anything to me. Save that for your interview with the head teacher.' Briana made her voice as soothing as possible. She had other ways of finding out what had happened without asking direct questions he could avoid. She needed to gain his trust first, which was going to take gentle handling and a bit of time, but she didn't have that luxury right now with a queue of kids waiting and a doctor gone AWOL right on clinic opening. Typical. They couldn't seem to get anyone to staff this clinic for longer than a term.

She gave Alfie a smile. 'I just need to know what kind of injury you have, where it hurts and if you need an X-ray and painkillers.'

Having ascertained his bruised jaw wasn't

fractured, she did a quick assessment of the rest of him. His hair was matted with mud, his black uniform trousers were torn and ragged at the knee, his school bag looked as if it had been dragged through cow dung. His hands were red and raw, fingernails ingrained with dirt, no doubt from where he'd landed after the punch to his chin. Great start to the term for this poor lad. He shrugged a scraggy shoulder. 'I'm fine.'

He wasn't fine, and his bottom lip was starting to wobble as the shock of the fight wore off.

Briana looked at the boy's reddened knuckles. 'Any pain in your hands?'

He made a sound she thought might be 'yes', then said, 'He said I was stupid. He said my sister's stupid too and told me what he was going to do with her down by the lake.' His face creased into an expression of pure disgust. 'I told him she's not a slut. That I'd punch his lights out if he said any more.'

'She must be proud to have a brother like you to stick up for her.'

No eye contact, head down, he spoke into his chest. 'She thinks I'm stupid too.'

'I bet she doesn't.'

'They both do. Just because they're two years older than me. That's not my fault, is it? Worse thing is, she loves him.' The boy shook his head in disbelief. 'How can she love someone who says things like that about her and hits her kid brother?'

Oh. Briana hadn't been expecting that.

'She doesn't know any better, Alfie. She's far too young and doesn't know what real love is. She thinks she does, but she's got a lot of growing up to do.'

You get drawn in, you fall too hard and too quickly, get taken in by their manipulation and before you know it, you're trapped.

Briana shoved her memories back. This was not the time to relive her own mistakes. 'Do you want me to have a word with her?'

He rolled his eyes. 'Tell her not to go out with Lewis Parker? Good luck with that, miss. She won't listen.'

'I won't actually say that, because you're right, she's not going to want to hear that from me. But I can have a gentle chat about relationship boundaries and expectations.' She smiled. 'Of course, I won't put it like that either. Lecturing people tends to put them off, right?'

'Right.' He nodded and his shoulders seemed to relax a little.

She tried a different tack. 'Lewis sounds like an annoying toddler. All that carrying on, trying to get attention.'

'Yeah.' His eyes brightened. 'Like my little sister. She won't shut up sometimes. She just makes a noise to get what she wants.'

'And how do you get her to stop?'

'Mum says if we ignore her, she'll just get bored.'

'And does she?'

'Yeah. I s'pose.' His expression became serious. 'You think I should do that with Lewis? Like, ignore him?'

'Do you think you can? It might help avoid a fight if you don't let him get to you.' Because they both knew Alfie was the one who'd hit out first. Trying to defend his sister, playing the tough guy. Saving face and family honour, even though he'd been provoked, because why else would a thirteen-year-old try his luck with someone two years older and a whole lot bigger? 'Often, ignoring them is the first thing you can do. But there are lots of other things too.'

She made a mental note to speak to Lewis Parker's form tutor as soon as she got the chance. Arming the victim as well as addressing the bad behaviour—or the underlying causes of the bad behaviour—often worked. What was going on in Lewis's life that made him need to bully others?

A sharp rap on the door had her turning round. It was Andrea, one of the school administrators. 'Sorry to interrupt, Briana, but I didn't know how long you were going to be—'

'I'm going, miss. Got to see Mr Wilson.' Alfie put the ice pack down and shouldered his school bag. The bruise on his chin was dark and swollen and he did not look happy about the prospect of seeing the head teacher.

'Okay, Alfie. Come back tomorrow morning so I can have a look at those bruises.' And check on his well-being. Arm him with more strategies.

With kids like Alfie, the best way of helping his emotional needs was to disguise it as dealing with his physical ones. Crafty, but it worked.

Andrea smiled as the boy dashed out of the door. 'The new doctor's here. I've done a walk-round to show him the layout and explained how the clinic works, but he's going to need the full Briana Barclay orientation.'

'As much as I know after only being here for a term.'

'You know more than him, that's always a start, right? Oh…' Andrea leaned closer and lowered her voice. 'Prepare yourself. He is hot, hot, hot.'

'Who? The new doctor that should have been here an hour ago? No one's hot when they can't be relied on to be on time.'

'To be fair, he said the email had confirmed a two-thirty start.' Andrea shrugged. 'Maybe he got it wrong? Can't have beauty *and* brains, right?'

'I don't care how good looking he is, if he isn't here on time to see the students they'll leave. It's hard enough to get them to attend appointments. They won't wait. They get the jitters, second-guess themselves and leave.'

'Did I mention he was hot?' Andrea fanned her face. Her cheeks were reddening, her eyes bright and dancing behind her reading glasses. She looked like a teenager swooning instead of a motherly fifty-something woman who should know better.

Bri laughed as she stalked into the waiting room with Andrea in her wake. 'Right, where is he? Let's get this over with. I have far more important things to do than mollycoddle a man—'

Oh, God. No.

'Bri…' Andrea was grinning and her eyes were wide, as if to say, *Ta-da! I present to you the hot new doctor.* 'This is Fraser Moore. Our new adolescent health specialist. All the way from London.'

He was standing in the middle of the room, filling it with his enigmatic presence and good-natured smile that she knew were just masking the real Fraser Moore. And, yes, she could see how Andrea might think him hot with his wide, haunting dark eyes. The short dark hair that was well groomed in a stylish city-boy look. The tan-coloured chinos and pale blue merino sweater that skimmed his rugged body. Oh, yes…she could see that someone who didn't know him would think him off-the-scale gorgeous, as she had done once upon a deluded time. Even the girls in the waiting room were staring at him as if a famous actor had just walked in.

But Bri knew better. She knew all about Fraser Moore.

Behind him a group of giggling girls burst into the waiting room. One of them stopped short, stared first at her then Fraser, her mouth gaping. She was about fifteen years old, hair pulled back into a long ponytail, dark eyes. She looked so familiar but Bri hadn't seen her around the school before.

Fraser's eyes widened and he looked guilty as hell, enough that Bri iintsinctively knew who this girl was.

Lily? Sweet, sweet Lily. Her heart lifted and hurt at the same time. All grown up with that teenager-going-on-twenty coquettishness.

All those missed years and missed chances.

Emotions hit her in the chest like bullets. Pain, sadness, rage, love. Bri's heart pounded, white noise filled her ears. She had no chance to gather herself and take stock. No chance to breathe. To try to drag on an expression that wasn't one of pure shock.

They lived here in the Lake District now?

Why? Fraser was a confirmed and devoted city man. When he'd visited years ago with Ellen and baby Lily he'd made it clear he couldn't breathe in all this space. Hated the crap public transport, the lack of buzz. The inward-looking parochialism of it all. So why here and why now?

And still Andrea was talking in her sugar-sweet voice, oblivious to the fact that the only hot things in the room right now were the daggers zipping between Bri and the man she'd hoped she'd never see again. 'Dr Fraser, this is our lovely school nurse, Briana Barclay.'

Briana closed her eyes and tried to stop her body from shaking. 'Fraser? What the actual hell are you doing here?'

The man who'd stolen the last few years of the most precious and dear friendship of her life. Who had prevented her from seeing her dying best friend in her last months of need. The man who'd blanked her and ghosted her. And now he was here to…what? To cause her pain? All over again?

Like hell he would.

CHAPTER TWO

'BRI. HI,' SAID FRASER, unsure how to act with someone who'd prefer it if he lived on the other side of the world. Or, in truth, didn't exist at all. And didn't even try to hide it. Hell, he hadn't exactly been expecting to see her either. He'd wondered if she might have moved back to the area but working with her in a school hadn't been remotely on his radar.

His presence here was going to take some explaining. Heart thumping hard against his chest wall, he tried for a smile. 'Surprise?'

She shook her head as her cheeks flushed, matching the silk blouse she was wearing. Red for danger. But he didn't need a sign to tell him he was on dodgy ground, her look said it all. As frosty as the mountains every morning since he'd been here. Her mouth flattened as her blue eyes narrowed. 'Please don't tell me you're living here now?'

'Um. I think I can hear my phone ringing. Got to go.' The administrator woman left the room and Fraser yearned to escape too. *Coward.* But there was no going back now.

'You remember Lily?' He beckoned to his daughter, who had just walked in and was staring at him as if he had two heads. He could feel the daggers in his back from her too. 'Lily, this is Briana. Your godmother. Not sure if you remember—'

'Duh. Briana's my middle name. Of course I remember her.' But Lily didn't look at all happy about meeting up with her godmother. In fact, she looked horrified.

'Oh, Lily, I can't believe how grown up you are.' Despite Lily's antagonistic expression Bri gave her a genuine smile and put her arms out, he imagined, for a hug, the way she'd done when Lily had been a little girl. Back then Lily would have toddled into her godmother's arms and hugged hard. They'd forged a strong bond in those early years as Lily grew up. Briana had been a regular visitor at Ellen's house and a keen babysitter when she could get time off work, but then Ellen had got sick and everything had gone to hell. Any bond between Lily and her godmother had been broken years ago.

Lily didn't move. 'Huh.'

Fraser hoped it was meant to be a 'hi' but had come out weirdly. He felt a need to explain everything to both of them, but not in front of the gawping audience. 'It's been a while since you saw each other.'

'Probably seven years, if you count all the time Ellen was sick and you didn't exactly encourage visiting,' Briana said, the smile fading back to the grim line, her arms dropping. 'Five years since…' She swallowed and blinked fast.

She didn't need to extrapolate. They both remembered the gut-wrenching heartache of the funeral, the way Briana had clamped her mouth shut but had said so much with her eyes. That somehow it had been his fault.

It had been a brain tumour. Not his fault, but he'd always wondered if he'd done the right things to ease Ellen's pain and the pain of those who loved her. He'd tried to protect his daughter from it all, but knew he hadn't, and wondered too whether the way he'd dealt with her mother's illness and death was the cause of Lily's subsequent issues.

Lily glared at him before giving a minute shake of her head. 'I'm going home. See you later.'

His heart squeezed. 'But we said we'd drive home together.'

'And now I'm going to get the bus.' Her eyes widened as they flicked to the teenagers sitting on the waiting-room chairs. *Shut up. Don't embarrass me.*

He'd already done her enough damage by

breathing the same air here, let alone having a stand-up confrontation with Briana.

'Lily, I'd love to catch up when you're free. I'm here most days, just pop down. Any time. Or maybe we could have a coffee sometime?' A mixture of emotions zipped across Briana's face. Her long blonde hair had been tied up in a messy bun and she had loose curls wisping round her face. She tucked one behind her ear as she pressed her lips together in a tight smile. She may have been shocked at finding them here, but there was hope in her gaze. She wanted a connection with Lily even after all these years.

It was a chink in her armour, and it gave him a little hope too. For the first time in a long time maybe he didn't have to do this all on his own. But that all depended on Lily, and he couldn't describe her reaction to all this as remotely positive.

'Uh, maybe.' Lily scuffed her shoe on the floor, not meeting Briana's eyes. Then she turned away from them both and walked to the door. 'I'm out of here.'

His heart hurt. But then it always did where his daughter was concerned.

The smile disappeared and Briana turned to him, her expression one of bitter pity.

'Still in the running for father of the month, I see?'

He breathed out deeply, wondering how much to confess and, deciding this wasn't the time or the place, he just went with, 'It's definitely a challenge.'

She rubbed her palms down her thighs, skimming fingers over her black trousers. 'Right. I have to go. We have students to see.'

'Could we talk? Later?'

'You and me? No way.' She grimaced and stepped back as if he'd struck her. 'But I would like to see Lily. We have a lot of catching up to do.'

He needed to explain why he'd acted the way he had back then. 'Bri. Please. I think we need to clear the air—'

'No, Fraser.' She looked as if she was about to explode, but she took a deep breath and gestured to the waiting room. 'I have a job to do.'

'As do I.' He backed off. This wasn't the time or place to talk through the past. 'But I haven't a clue where to start. Andrea said you'd show me around. I'm pretty sure some of the processes will be different from London. I don't want to stuff up on my first day.'

'You already have.' She sighed and shook her head, the red on her cheeks less intense but the glittering anger in her eyes still very much in situ. But she nodded. 'Follow me.'

They crossed the busy waiting area to a door that said 'Clinic Two' on it. She opened it, went in, waiting for him to follow her, and then closed the door, all professional and aloof. 'This is your clinic room. On the desk is a file of information on local providers, but if you've used the EMIS system before you'll know how to find specialists in the area. If you'd arrived a decent amount of time before clinic started, I could have shown you properly. Now you'll have to whizz through the best way you can.

'It's the first day of term so I'm not expecting much more than what we have waiting out there, but you never know what's going to come in through the door. Any problems, call me. Extension 556 on the internal phone. Clinic One.'

'Briana, I'm sorry.'

'For what exactly? Being late? Being here at all? Putting yourself in between me and my best friend when she was *dying*?' She swallowed then held a trembling hand up just as he was about to explain. 'I don't have time for this, Fraser.'

'The email said two-thirty.'

'Then it was wrong.'

And with that she slammed the door behind her.

So, that hadn't gone as well as he'd hoped.

Nausea ate at him during each consultation throughout the afternoon.

Had he made a massive error of judgement by bringing Lily here? Hell, he'd been wondering that ever since they'd packed the car with their belongings and headed north. But being a parent was all about protecting, guiding and keeping your kids safe.

He'd hoped Bri might have been accepting, welcoming even, but he should have known better. She'd been hurt and angry and she blamed him. Well, hell, she had good cause to. If only she'd let him explain, but that needed time and probably some alcohol to ease the way.

After he finished typing up the last patient's notes he pulled on his winter coat and wandered through to the waiting room.

It was empty. The place smelled of gym shoes and the overwhelming cloying sweetness of cheap body spray that teenagers were so keen to cover themselves in. Posters clung to the walls, curling at the edges, with myriad health messages about pregnancy testing, sexually transmitted disease, anti-bullying.

Nothing to help parents with teenagers who wouldn't talk or listen.

And no Briana Barclay to be seen. He wasn't sure whether to knock on her door, wait or just leave, but suddenly her door swung open and she walked out, carrying a large pile of papers and folders. The second she caught sight of him she frowned and stopped.

He decided it was going to take time to smooth things out between them, so he found her a smile, hoping it looked genuine. 'I'll be off, then.'

'How did you go?'

'Slowly. It's hard with only fifteen-minute appointments. I'm used to longer. I like to be thorough.'

'We can make them longer.' A curt nod. 'What do you need?'

'Twenty at least? Let's see how that goes. I know it's luxury to want that much but I do think we get better outcomes if we give our clients the time they need.'

'Anything I need to know about?'

That it wasn't all *my fault. That I need some help. That the last few years have been so bloody hard.*

And with no siblings or parents able or willing to help, Bri might be his only salvation. For Lily's sake. *And Ellen's.*

'Mostly straightforward. Things of note—one kid wanting to bulk up, asking for...' he made quote marks in the air with his fingers '..."legit steroids".' He laughed. 'I put him right about that and suggested a personal weight training plan I've used in the past with good results. A gender identity consultation, which I think is going to take a few more sessions to ascertain appropriate pathways—'

'The nearest gender identity clinic is in Leeds.'

'Yes, I scoped that out. I don't know if we're at the referral stage yet, so I suggested some websites they can look at, some questions to think about and booked another appointment next week. I'm hoping one of the parents might come in too at some point so we can have a family chat. Everything else was straightforward.'

'Good. Sounds like you managed.'

'I did. Do you schedule pastoral team meetings so we can discuss cases in more depth?'

'Yes. I should have given you this.' She pulled out a file from the pile of papers in her hands and gave it to him. 'Proper orientation information. Hours we work, multi-disciplinary meeting timetables, that kind of thing. We talk with the counsellors and pastoral care staff once a month. It's all in there. Oh, and I owe you an apology.'

Interesting. Hope rose in his chest. 'Yes?'

'Looks like Andrea inadvertently told you to come at two-thirty. Should have been an hour earlier.' She turned and made her way to the door, her back straight and her shoulders taut. Her body thrummed with annoyance and he could tell she was hurrying to get away from him.

That was an apology? He wasn't going to argue the toss, but in his world apologies started or ended with *I'm sorry*.

Not exactly the kind of step in the right direction he was hoping for, but it was a start. He owed her an apology too. 'Briana, I didn't know you were going to be working here.'

She whirled round to look at him. Her eyes were large and a startling, glittering blue. Close up he could see hues of gold in there too. He'd never noticed that before. But, then, she'd been his ex-girlfriend's best friend. Very off limits, which meant he hadn't gone looking too hard.

Her lips were full and she'd put gloss on, making them shimmer. His eyes seemed to be drawn there. Weird. And totally inappropriate, smack-bang in the middle of an argument with a work colleague and kind of old friend, who hated him.

He dragged his gaze back to her eyes.

He knew from the years of her friendship with Ellen that Briana was fiercely loyal, often outrageously funny and loved deeply, but she was far from those now and the tone of her words was dark. 'Really, Fraser? I find it odd that you just turn up on my patch. It can't possibly be a coincidence. If I remember rightly, you're not a big fan of the great outdoors. You prefer bars and clubs and music, not mountains and lakes and birdsong.'

'People change. Parenting tends to curb the late nights and loud music, as does holding down a demanding job.'

'People don't change that much.' Her eyes narrowed. 'It's not as if you have any relatives here. What's the real story?'

Even though she had every right to be angry with him her words were like shrapnel piercing him. Everything he'd done had been to protect Lily and Ellen and he knew he'd hurt Briana in the process, but he'd made a promise and he wasn't going to apologise for that.

'We needed to get out of London. I hoped fresh air and climbing mountains might help so when I saw the job advert for Oakdale Medical Centre with two afternoons a week doing outreach it seemed like the perfect opportunity.' And yet here it was, far from perfect right now.

'But you knew I grew up here, went to school here with Ellen. Surely there was a chance I might be here?'

'To be honest, I had no idea where you were. We got Lily's birthday and Christmas cards from Australia a few years ago. And then…we didn't know where you'd gone.' The presents and cards had trickled to a stop and Briana had slipped from Lily's mind. Fraser's, too, until recently.

'I was in Australia, yes. Four and a bit years. I should have sent her more, I know.' Bri shook her head in a way that didn't invite further questioning.

'I did email you about this job. Three times. I asked whether you knew anything about it. I asked if you were okay with us coming here and if we could try to patch things up for Lily's sake. You never replied.' He shrugged, watching as his words hit home, her expression softening as he explained. 'I figured you'd either decided never to speak to us again, or I'd landed in your junk email box or—'

'I… I changed my email address.' She blinked fast and looked suddenly embarrassed. Good, it was a relief to have the heat shift from him for a change. Their friendship breakdown hadn't all been his fault, although he knew he was definitely the main culprit.

'And you didn't think to let me…let Lily know?'

She looked down, biting her bottom lip. 'I was going to.'

'Well, I've saved you the bother.'

'I was going to.' She met his gaze. 'Lily's my goddaughter and I want to be there for her.'

Five years too late.

'By changing your email address.'

She closed her eyes. 'I had my reasons.'

'Which were?'

'Private.' She folded her arms across her chest in a gesture that was pure panic, as if she was protecting herself and turning her thoughts inward. She was guarded and so unlike the Briana he remembered from years ago. Sure, he'd expected her outburst. That was how she was. She'd worn her heart on her sleeve back then. She didn't generally tiptoe around and she believed wholeheartedly in being honest—he knew that to his cost.

There'd always been tension between them, a spark of…something. Irritation, maybe. Jealousy, perhaps, that he'd been Ellen's man. He'd always felt she was judging him, that he wasn't good enough for her friend. But he hadn't walked away from Ellen, and he'd made sure he was accessible and reliable and a damned good father.

He wasn't sure what had caused Briana's sudden shutdown and he didn't like the way it made her so guarded, but she clearly wasn't going to tell him anything more. She turned away, rubbing her arms. They'd reached an impasse.

She bent and straightened the files on the reception desk, not looking at him, but her hands were shaking, and he wasn't sure whether it was the shock of seeing him and Lily or for the reason she'd changed her email address.

'I tried, Briana. I didn't want it to happen this way.'

'I've heard that before too.' She shook her head in a gesture reminiscent of his teenage daughter, as if to say, *Whatever.* 'You still haven't explained why you upped sticks and moved here, precisely. Ellen's dad died a couple of years ago and her mum's been gone a long time. Why not go to your mother's if you needed to move?'

'Mum moved to Portugal a few years ago. She did come and help out for a while after Ellen died, but Lily was too much for her. She's retired now and finally living a life she enjoys, rather than scraping by like she had to when she brought me up. I couldn't ask her for more help.' It wasn't as if she'd ever relished playing mother to him anyway and, in fact, blamed him for his father leaving her. So he was on his own. As usual.

Bri's eyebrows rose. 'So, you have no other connection to the Lake District as far as I know. Surely there must have been other GP jobs you could have taken somewhere else in England?'

'Full time but flexible with a side serving of adolescent outreach? Far away from London? Not many. I jumped at the first opportunity. And, well…' Confession time. 'I did hope you and Lily might connect at some point.'

'Why?'

He tried for a smile, but wasn't sure he managed it as the truth of his words hit him square in the chest. 'Desperation?'

'Typical, Fraser.' Her arms folded tight across her chest. 'The only time you'd even consider me is when you're desperate.'

Frustration bubbled up. 'Are you deliberately misinterpreting me? That's not what I meant—'

The door banged open and the administrator stood there, red-faced and breathing hard. 'Sorry to interrupt, but there's been an incident at football training and they need help.'

Fraser's words stuck in his throat. He glanced at Briana. She was still shaking with anger. Her eyes sparked and glittered and he was drawn to look at her again.

She was so striking, beautiful, in fact, yet he'd never noticed before.

The school administrator looked from one to the other, eyebrows raised and a curious look on her face, as if she'd caught them snogging behind the bike sheds or something.

Not bloody likely.

She held the door open. 'I mean…they need help. Like *now*.'

CHAPTER THREE

WAS IT BAD that a boy in pain was a welcome distraction from Fraser Moore?

Probably. But right now Briana was grateful for the respite from all the feelings he instilled in her.

She grabbed the first-aid kit, ran through the school corridors and out towards the sports fields, where a huddle of boys was crowded around dark shapes on the ground. It was dark outside and the freezing northerly bit her cheeks and sheared deep into her bones. She wished she'd had the foresight to grab her coat.

There'd been no more time to talk, but she'd felt Fraser behind her every step and now he was pushing his way through to the boy—no, *boys*, three of them, on the frosted ground. Moans filled the air.

He knelt down on the frozen playing field, looking from one kid to another and then another, no doubt assessing who need the most urgent attention. He went first to a boy lying prone. Eyes closed. Not moving.

'Hey, there.' Fraser's voice was calm and friendly and belied the rush of urgency that must have been spinning inside him at seeing an un-moving child splayed on the earth. 'I'm the new doctor. Can someone tell me what happened?'

'Ball in the air. Head clash.' A teenager hold-ing his hand to a split lip pointed to the uncon-scious boy, then to himself and lastly to another kid moaning on the ground, clutching his leg. 'Bad landing.'

Bri looked at the chaos, assessed the damage and fished her phone from her pocket. 'Has any-one called an ambulance?'

'Er...' The boys looked at each other. 'We told Mrs Walker.'

Andrea. And she'd come to get them. 'Right. Good call.' Bri watched as Fraser did an airways assessment on the unconscious boy, who was, thankfully, breathing independently and start-ing to move his head. His eyes flickered open, then closed again as he told them his name was Connor.

Bri exchanged glances with Fraser and he said, 'Glasgow Coma scale twelve.'

Not life-threatening, but definitely worrying—and at risk of hypothermia if they stayed here much longer.

'On it.' She made the call to the ambulance service, then focused on the moaning teenager who was clutching his lower leg. Josh Parker, Briana recognised him—always in the sick bay with some sort of sporting injury. 'It hurts.'

'I'm sure it does. Can I take a look?' She peeled the boy's hands away from his leg and squinted, not seeing well in the dark. 'Can someone shine a light here, please?'

One of the kids whipped out a phone, swiped for the flashlight then recoiled. 'Ugh. Is that the bone sticking out?'

Yes, the bone is right there. A nasty compound fracture. 'This is going to need more than just a bandage. I'll dial in to ambulance HQ again and ask for reinforcements.' She tried to make light of it so as not to spook the already anxious-looking kids. 'You guys don't do things by halves.'

When she finished the second phone call she heard split lip boy—Henry, in the school blue and white football strip—talking to Fraser in a wobbly voice. 'We were both running for the ball, jumping up at the same time and…we hit our heads. He was out cold.' The kid swallowed, his voice breaking. 'It was an accident. All of it.'

'It…was.' Josh was rolling on the ground in pain, shivering from shock and cold.

'It's okay, no one's in trouble.' She stroked Josh's hair out of his eyes and handed him a tissue from the first-aid kit, then wrapped him in her cardigan.

Next, she took a look at Henry's lip, cleaning it the best she could with some saline and gauze.

'I don't think it needs stitches. Make sure you give it a good rinse out when you get home just to wash all the dirt out. Might hurt to eat for the next day or two, but I've heard how much teenage boys eat and I don't think a little cut is going to put you off, right?' She winked and gave him some sterile swabs to press on to the lip to stem the bleeding. 'You want me to call your parents?' Bri took the names and numbers and made more calls, the cold now starting to seep into her bones.

'We need to keep everyone warm. It's freezing,' Fraser said as he looked at her with concern. 'You're shivering.'

'I'm fine.' She didn't want him to think she couldn't cope.

Even though the cloudy night sky had started to dump sleet on them, Fraser peeled off his thick coat and wrapped it over his patient's skinny frame. Moving Connor would have been too dangerous in case there was a neck injury, but they had to keep him warm somehow, and still.

Briana watched as Fraser moved languidly and confidently and, for one split second—definitely not more—she felt a frisson of something familiar firing back into life deep inside her. She couldn't take her eyes away from the half-smile on his lips as he reassured Connor, the deft way he supported the boy's head. Kind eyes that drew you in.

No.

She wasn't going to start mooning over Fraser again. *Been there, done that.*

She refused to allow it. No way. Definitely not. For so many reasons. Her anger at him, of course. But mainly because back when she'd had her inconvenient crush on him all those years ago he'd barely even acknowledged she'd existed. She certainly wasn't going to start chasing that particular line of thought again.

She cleared her throat and ignored the annoying fluttering in her belly. 'Can someone grab a couple of blankets from the sick bay?' At least they had plenty of hands to help.

Soon enough she had them all wrapped up warmly, except Henry, who refused the blanket and hovered over Connor, concern etched deep in his features, along with guilt. 'Is he going to be okay?'

Connor was starting to come round. His eyes were open and Fraser was getting the boy to squeeze his hands, assessing strength and sensation, and looking for any weaknesses. He moved to the boy's feet, ran his fingers over the ankle bones. It looked as if there was no serious neck or back injury that affected his limbs but they both knew he would need a thorough hospital assessment after a head-clash that had knocked him out cold.

'I'm sure he will be, mate.' Fraser looked up at Henry and smiled. 'Look, I need someone I can trust to go out to the front of the school and direct the ambulance round to us. Can you do that?'

The boy nodded slowly. 'Sure.'

'Great. They won't be long.'

'Good call.' Bri nodded as Henry walked away. 'He needs to feel useful.'

'I know. I've been in the same situation. You get embroiled in something that ends up hurting someone else. You feel like hell, even if it isn't your fault.' His eyes caught her gaze and she wondered if he was trying to tell her something.

She turned away, not wanting to hear it.

The parents and the ambulances all seemed to arrive at the same time in a blur of sirens and headlights. While Briana spoke to the parents Fraser assisted the ambulance staff with Connor, log-rolling him onto a stretcher and keeping his neck stabilised.

Josh's leg was immobilised by an inflatable splint, he was given pain relief before his journey to hospital and his mum went with him in the second ambulance.

Briana was right, Henry's lip didn't need stitches, but Fraser wrote a prescription for antibiotics in case the wound started to look infected— a possible complication owing to the prevalence of mud on the boy—and made Henry's parents promise to make an appointment at the Oakdale Medical Centre if they were worried.

One by one the other team members and their

parents left and Fraser spent a couple of minutes talking to the paramedics.

He looked genuinely concerned about Connor's head injury and the long-term implications of concussion, and Briana was impressed with the way that they'd handled the situation as a team. Nothing like a medical emergency to smooth things over and make them forget—or at least put aside—their differences.

For now.

But Briana hadn't forgotten how Fraser could be. She would never forget that he'd put a barrier between her and her best friend. Or forgive him.

There was nothing more for her to do here and she could have just left but that seemed churlish and rude after what they just shared. She decided to stay, if only to thank him for his help.

He was taking his time, so it wasn't exactly her fault if she let her eyes wander across that broad chest. *Hmm.* He'd changed from the last time she'd seen him, although admittedly that had been at a funeral. He'd been thin then. Eaten up with the stress of looking after Ellen and his daughter. No doubt made worse by Briana's railing at him…but he'd deserved it.

Five years on, he'd filled out, added muscle where muscle looked very nice on a man: arms, butt, thighs. Eyes that mirrored his emotions.

He wanted to patch things up for Lily's sake and that had to be good.

Her *goddaughter*. Guilt rippled through her. She should have stayed in London, should have helped, forced herself into their world. But Hurricane Tony had happened and she'd been blinded by her feelings for him, eaten up with grief at Ellen's death, and angry at Fraser. She'd needed space to deal with all the overwhelming emotion that had threatened to almost drown her and Lily had somehow got lost in the mix.

Although not in Fraser's world. He'd taken care of his little girl, always put her first. So what had happened to make him uproot her and take her away from everything she knew?

She needed to befriend Lily, take her godmother duties seriously and be an advocate for her. Not ogle him inappropriately. He'd been her best friend's man and that was a line not to be crossed.

'That was certainly a bit of excitement for my first day.' They'd fallen into step with each other, walking to the staff car park. He headed towards an old battered Volvo that looked like it had seen better days. Interesting. She'd imagined the city boy to have something a lot more flash than that.

She zapped the automatic lock on her little silver runabout. 'Thank you for the help. I'll see you on Wednesday.'

But he didn't look like he was in a hurry to leave. Instead of opening his car door, he stopped, turned to look at her and said, 'I'm sorry about the way Lily reacted.'

He did indeed look genuinely sorry. And, yes, having watched him kneel on the icy ground, not caring about his chinos or about getting his hands dirty, or about anything except the injured child in front of him, she had to admit he was climbing back up the hot scales. For Briana, hotness levels were definitely linked to compassion levels and closely aligned to sense of humour levels. Not so much the physical—although he had that in spades—but how a man made her feel.

Fraser Moore made her feel too many things. 'I take it you didn't tell her I was here?'

'I didn't want to get her hopes up in case you weren't. She's not usually like that...' He paused. Ran fingers through his sleet-damp hair. 'Actually, she is. She's changed, Bri. From that sweet little girl into someone I don't recognise.'

'Kids grow up, it's not always a smooth ride and you know that. You have to give her some leeway to find her own path. Loosen the reins.'

'I did. It didn't work out. I tightened them and that didn't work either. Now we're here and she's worse. She says I'm punishing her when I'm just trying to help.'

'Moving her away from her friends and everything, she knows isn't punishing her? Controlling her?'

'*Loving* her. Protecting her. There is a difference.'

'Yes, I've heard it called that too. So many times. *"But he loves me... Even though he won't let me see my friends... But he cares for me."* That's not how you love someone, Fraser. You set them free. You support them. You—'

His eyes were dark now. 'Let them get a criminal record?'

Whoa. She hadn't been expecting that. 'What do you mean?'

He let out a long sigh and she could see he was choosing his words. 'Lily was caught shoplifting with a bunch of her so-called friends. Just some cheap make-up, but enough to be taken to the police station. I managed to convince them not to press charges and paid the store a lot of money to make it all go away.'

'It happens, Fraser. It's not right, but it happens. She's just being a kid, pushing boundaries.'

His eyes closed for a moment, then, 'There were other things too. One of her friends has been charged with possession of drugs. Another for dealing. At fifteen, Bri. No matter what I said or did, it didn't seem to make a difference. I couldn't stop her seeing these people unless I locked her up. Which, for the record, I did not do. Even when I grounded her, she'd climb out of the window at night and hang out with them. Brought back by the police in the early hours. Not just once.

I don't know if she ever took drugs and I doubt she'd ever tell me. She's already on a police caution, Briana.' He looked distraught. 'What next?'

Oh, God. Poor Fraser. Poor Lily.

'I didn't realise it was so bad.'

'How could you know?' He shook his head. The unsaid *you weren't there* hung between them. 'I'm not controlling her, I'm protecting her, taking her out of harm's way.'

The threat of a criminal record must have been a very big wake-up call. She was starting to understand what had driven him to bring his daughter all this way away from everything she knew. A fresh start. Lily deserved that after what she'd been through in her short life. Losing a mother would have been so hard. And for her best friend's sake Bri need to help.

Help Lily. Her goddaughter. Make up for all that lost time. Yes. She could do that.

And if that meant spending more time with Fraser, then so be it. She'd just have to put up with him.

Admiring his body hadn't meant anything.

Even with all this new information and the way he'd looked when he'd talked about his daughter—with such pain and raw love and compassion aplenty—he still most definitely wasn't her kind of hot.

CHAPTER FOUR

'You didn't think to mention my godmother works at my new school? Some advance warning would have been nice.'

Lily was sitting at the dinner table in their kitchen/dining room, simultaneously growling at her father whilst hugging Jasper, their Old English sheepdog, the only bribery Fraser had resorted to in an attempt to smooth the house move.

We can get a dog.

So, of course, she'd chosen the biggest, clumsiest, smelliest, fur-shedding dog she could find. One that broke china with a swift whack of its tail, made muddy prints and drool trails across the slate floor tiles on a daily basis and who thought it was a human, so tried to sit with them at the dinner table. Every. Day.

But Lily loved him. That was something.

It was just a shame the love didn't extend as far as mopping up the trails or replacing the china, but there it was.

Fraser stirred the bolognaise sauce and tried

not to rise to another argument. 'I didn't know Briana worked there. I didn't know she's a school nurse. But…' he did concede, because he believed in honesty '… I did know she grew up near here, like your mum. So we may possibly have bumped into her at some point. Look, I emailed her about us moving here and she didn't reply, so I assumed she was still in Australia. I didn't see the point in saying anything to you if we weren't going to see her. What's the problem with her being here?'

Lily grimaced. 'You have spies everywhere, right? Here in cosy little Oakdale, where you can't turn around without bumping into someone who knows your business. And now at school too. I can't have any privacy. Not to mention the fact you had the big reunion showdown in front of everyone.'

'Ah. Yes. Sorry about that. It didn't exactly go the way I'd imagined it might. How was school? Have you made any friends yet?'

'I was trying to, you know. I was hanging out with a couple of girls from one of my classes and one of them had a headache, so we went to the sick bay for painkillers. But—well, you know the rest.' She glared at him. 'Bit hard to make friends with your father arguing with the school nurse right in front of you.'

His gut tightened. 'I'm sorry, Lily.'

'Really?' She buried her nose into Jasper's fur.

'My lovely boy. You're the only one who under-stands me.'

The dog looked up at her with those killer big eyes and put his paw on her knee.

'I love you.' She nuzzled Jasper's head and the pang of affection and despair in Fraser's chest almost stopped his breath.

When had she last said that to him? Certainly not this side of the Great Move North. Probably not for a year, or two. The damned shame of it all was that she desperately craved affection and attention, but she didn't want it from him.

Dinner was a sombre affair that involved Lily moving food around her plate and Fraser trying to make jokes that she didn't laugh at. Just as they finished there was a knock on the door and they both looked up. Lily shrugged. 'Won't be for me.'

Fraser went through to the hall and opened the door. A blast of freezing air and thick snowflakes blew in as he peered out. To his surprise, Briana was standing there, her blonde hair in loose curls around her shoulders and flecked with snow-flakes. She had a pale blue scarf wrapped round her neck above a navy corduroy jacket, figure-hugging jeans and boots. She looked ten years younger than she had in her work clothes—back to the young woman he remembered. And a little nervous. His gut did a weird jig, tightening again but for a very different reason.

It really needed to stop doing that.

She smiled. 'Hey.'

'This is a surprise.' He stepped back to let her in, strangely relieved and intrigued that she was here.

'Is this convenient?' She walked into the hallway and popped a large handbag on the floor while she shook the snow from her jacket. 'I've come to see Lily.'

Of course she had. His ego took a hit on that. *Idiot.*

Why he'd thought she was here to see him he couldn't say. And why he felt deflated was even more of a mystery. He walked her through to the lounge where Lily was lying on her back next to Jasper on the floor, her legs propped up on the sofa as she talked animatedly on the phone.

'As soon as I can. I promise. I've checked the train timeta— Oh.' She twisted upright when she saw Fraser and then Briana, her eyes rolling. 'Later,' Lily said into the phone and hurriedly slipped it into her pocket.

'Hi, Lily.' Briana waved. No big hugging gesture. He assumed she'd learnt the first time. But she didn't look abashed, just friendly. Casual. 'Just wondered how you're settling in?'

Lily shrugged.

Bri nodded. 'It's a pretty relaxed school and, between you and me, it's the best place for Wi-Fi signal in the area.'

Lily's eyes widened. 'It's rubbish here.'

'Same at my house. It's all the mountains.' Bri shrugged. 'My movie streaming is so slow I get that swirling circle of doom on my screen every time.'

Lily shot her a look that suggested she couldn't imagine Bri knowing what streaming was. Then she looked back at her phone as if it was the answer to all of her woes.

'Well, as long as you're okay. First days are always daunting.' Briana watched her, then slowly took a large book out of her bag. 'Before I forget, I've brought some photos to show you guys. Thought you might like to see what Ellen got up to growing up around here.'

'Er…' Lily's eyes darted to her dad and then back to Briana. She looked like a caged animal searching for an escape route. 'It's just… I have… er, homework.'

Fraser frowned. Homework she hadn't mentioned yet?

'Hey, no problem. I wasn't going to stay. Just thought I'd drop them off for you to have a look later.' Briana put the album on the coffee table, her smile fading a little, and he could see her work to bring it back to full wattage as she bent and patted Jasper, who promptly drooled on her shoes. She grimaced then looked at Lily. 'He's gorgeous. What's his name?'

'Jasper. But Dad calls him a pain in the ar—'

'Lily.' He growled, but Briana laughed. 'He's the most handsome boy I've ever seen.'

'Yes. He is.' A little hitch in Lily's voice and for a second her eyes softened, then she turned and walked to the door. 'Homework.'

Bri nodded. 'Have they got you working on your first day? That's just mean.'

'Yep.'

Exasperated with Lily's monosyllabic responses, Fraser took up Briana's cause. 'Lily. Come and have a look at the photos.'

But his daughter had disappeared with exaggerated thuds up the ancient narrow steps of their stone cottage, followed by the swish swish of her faithful Jasper climbing the stairs behind her.

Fraser found himself apologising for his daughter. Again. 'I'm so sorry, Bri. I'll call her back down. She can't be rude like that.'

Briana blinked. 'It's fine. I don't expect her to want to spend time with me. I'm pretty much a stranger in her life. Making her come down isn't going to be pleasant for any of us.'

'She needs to learn her manners.'

She raised her palm. 'Hey, I totally believe you'll have taught her how to behave properly, Fraser. Don't worry.'

'I have talked about you. She does remember you.'

'It's okay. Honestly. It's a lot for her to take in.' She started to walk towards the door. 'I just thought I'd pop by. It's going to take time for her to get used to me again.'

He felt bad that she'd come all that way only to have the full-on rude Lily reception, and he wanted to make amends for…everything. 'Wait, Bri. Do you want stay for a drink? Glass of wine?'

She shook her head. 'I should go.'

'I remember you like a glass of red.' He held up a bottle of merlot to tempt her. 'It'll be nice to have adult company for a change…someone who isn't going to flounce off in a strop or tell me I'm embarrassing every time I open my mouth.'

'Picked the wrong woman here, then.' She laughed, although he wasn't sure if he imagined the hint of bitterness there too.

He shrugged, feigning nonchalance even though the thought of having a glass of wine with someone was off-the-scale good. 'I'll take my chances.'

'I've been working on my flouncing. I've reached expert level.' Her eyebrows rose wryly. 'But, for the record, you're not embarrassing *every* time you open your mouth.'

He liked the sparring. 'There's a relief.'

'Just ninety-nine-point-nine percent of the time,' she threw at him with a chuckle.

But she didn't leave.

He took a couple of glasses from the oak dresser and waggled them in front of her. 'I think we need to clear the air. From a work perspective, if nothing else.'

She thought about it for a moment and he wondered what was going on in her head. Her eyes darted from the glass to him and then back. Eventually she shrugged. 'Okay. We need to talk from a Lily perspective too. I promised both you and Ellen that I'd be there for her, and I haven't been.'

'The promises we keep, eh? Get you into trouble if you're not careful.'

Her back stiffened. 'Fraser, I'm not ready to go over that yet.'

He wasn't sure he'd ever be ready but he needed to explain. 'Bri, we can't ignore it.'

'Not today, please.' She rubbed her head. 'It's all a bit much, to be honest. Seeing you and Lily brought so many memories back. I'm still processing.'

'Okay. Another time. Sit, please. I think that seat is dog-hair-free, but I can't be sure.' His heart thumped as he indicated for her to sit on the sofa. That old ground would have to wait. He'd have to reassure her that he hadn't wanted to lie. That he hadn't been playing mind-games. But that was for another time.

He poured two glasses of wine, unsure what they were going to talk about if they weren't ready to talk about the elephant in the room. 'Sorry about the drool.'

Awkward.

'Oh?' She followed his gaze to her shoes where a sticky spill oozed over her laces. 'Not a problem.'

'Occupational hazard when you've got a dog like that. Big dog, big mess.'

Just like Fraser's attempt at conversation.

This was not going well. Searching for some common ground that wasn't going to erupt in an argument, he picked up the photo album. 'I bet there are some photos in here I haven't seen before.'

'These are from when Ellen and I met at nursery, right up until we left here to go do our nurse training together and I think there might be some of that night we met you at the hospital Christmas ball.' She gestured for him to come and sit next to her as she showed him pictures of two small girls—one dark haired, one blonde, playing at a beach, at a park, in the school concert. On the Windermere ferry, eating ice creams, on the top of a mountain. Girls growing up together, sharing secrets and having fun. Then photos of older girls with straightened hair and make-up, wearing ballgowns.

His heart tripped as he looked at Ellen, so full of life and with so much to look forward to.

Briana ran her fingertip across the photo. 'Imagine…if we hadn't been at that ball, you and I wouldn't even know each other. Lily wouldn't even exist.'

Another photo, this time of Ellen and Briana inside the ball venue, holding glasses of bubbly up to the camera. Then a picture he hadn't even known was being taken of Ellen, Briana and himself. Briana grinning at the camera, he and Ellen grinning at each other under a sprig of plastic mistletoe.

It had been lust at first sight. He, a medical student on a rare night off and letting off steam with his friends, and Ellen, a beautiful, bright student nurse—they'd bumped into each other at the bar, shared some hilarious, lecherous conversation and a few jokes, danced until their feet ached and then spent the night…

He wasn't sure what had happened to Briana after the music ended, he'd been so wrapped up in Ellen.

'Shame the band was so bad,' he said, just to break the heavy silence as they lost themselves in their memories.

'We were just excited to be glammed up and going out after spending weeks studying.' She quickly turned the page to find more photos of them, this time the girls on another rare day off sightseeing in Covent Garden. She peered closer. 'What the hell were we wearing? Oh, God. Look at us.' She slammed her palm over the print. 'No! Forget that! Do not look at us.'

'It can't be anything I haven't seen before.' He

snatched the book from her and held it high above his head so she couldn't grab it from him.

She reached out to get it, but didn't manage. Although she put up a good fight, stretching, giggling, groaning. 'Don't you dare laugh, Fraser Moore. I took my clothing choices very seriously at eighteen.'

'I'm not going to be responsible for my reactions.' Intrigued, he turned his back on her and opened the album, relieved that the atmosphere had morphed into something almost friendly. *Almost*, given the elephant she refused to talk about. 'Let me see. Oh, yes. Ah. I see what you mean. Got to love the naughty noughties.' He couldn't stop the laughter escaping even though her cheeks burned. But she was laughing too, her eyes dancing and bright. Her smile radiant.

Something caught in his chest as he watched her. How had he never realised how pretty she was? How…*attractive*?

She reached and laughed and her gaze caught with his. As she looked at him his body prickled hotly.

No. She'd always been off limits. Still was. This weird feeling inside him was just a giddy relief that they could manage a semblance of communication.

Possibly, also, because he was sharing some time with a level-headed grown-up.

She reached for the album. 'Please, Fraser. I

am dying here. I'd forgotten that was in there.
You can see my—'

The door swung open and Lily flounced in,
eyes narrowed in suspicion. 'I thought I heard…
laughing.'

It sounded like an accusation. As if laughter
wasn't allowed. Okay, so it had been missing for
a long time, but he ached for more of it, to see
his daughter's rare smile.

Briana pointed to the photograph, the laughter
less but the humour still in her voice. Her cheeks
had bloomed hot pink and he wondered if she'd
felt that zip of electricity too. 'Oh, Lily. This probably should be X-rated, but what the hell? You're
old enough not to be scarred for life. Have a look
and learn from our mistakes. Whoever thought
thong knickers and low-rise jeans were a good
fashion statement?'

Lily leaned in to look, a faint smile playing at
the corners of her mouth, but she pressed her lips
together as if willing herself not to laugh.

Poor Lily. Wouldn't allow herself to be seen to
be having fun.

Still laughing, Briana put the album on the coffee table, open at the offending picture. 'Those
were the days, eh?'

He chanced another look at Briana. When she
forgot to be cross with him she was enchanting,
disarming.

But she was looking at Lily now. 'Let that be

a lesson to you, Lily. Don't be fooled by trendy ideas.'

Lily looked shocked, but also surprised. She laughed. Actually laughed. 'Don't worry. I actually do have fashion sense.'

'Unlike us, back then. We didn't have a clue. You know, you look so much like her. Especially when you laugh.' Bri touched her heart with her palm and her voice cracked as she spoke. 'You have her eyes. All dark and sparkly.'

'My mum's?' Lily blinked. Swallowed.

'Yes. You have Ellen's eyes and smile. She was so pretty and funny. Sometimes a bit ditzy. Not exactly the most organised of people.'

Chaos, Fraser was about to add, *delightful chaos*, but decided to keep his mouth shut. Besides, he wasn't sure he could force words out of his lumpy throat. He rubbed at the pain in his chest as if it might go away with a bit of pressure. Truth was, the pressure had often been intense, and the pain always remained.

'We were always running out of milk.' Lily smiled at the memory, clearly enchanted to be talking about her mum. 'I used to make her write lists or she'd just forget things.'

'You and me both.' Bri laughed. 'She was so not a list person. But she was such fun to be around no one cared.'

'She was.' Lily glanced at the photo album. Then slid sideways onto one of the armchairs, her long legs dangling over the arm, and casually flicked the album to face her. Then she glanced at it. And away again. Trying not to show interest when she was clearly intrigued.

'There's a photo of her when she was about your age. Peas in a pod.' Briana pushed the book closer to Lily.

Lily flicked the album open at the beginning and slowly looked through the photos. Briana gave her a gentle commentary explaining when and where they had all been taken, going over Ellen's life in much more detail than he probably could. He'd learned a lot about his ex over the years, but as their romantic relationship had been a flash of lust that had fizzled out just as quickly, they hadn't done the whole needing to learn every little thing about each other. They'd probably have never seen each other again had Ellen not discovered she was pregnant.

They'd agreed to co-parent, that a romantic relationship wasn't what either of them wanted, but they'd both adored Lily and the three of them had developed a tight bond, an unconventional family that had lived only streets apart and that had worked. Until Ellen had become too sick to look after herself, never mind her daughter, so she'd moved in with him and he'd ended up as carer to both females in his life.

When Bri closed the book, Lily jumped up. It was hard to read his daughter's expression. For a few minutes she'd been engrossed in the stories but she didn't look comfortable now. She edged towards the door.

His stomach tensed. Dealing with his teenager was like walking a tightrope. One false move and he was spiralling into despair. But he knew he just had to keep holding on.

Briana looked at him worriedly, eyebrows raised in a silent question… *Is she okay?*

He stood too and managed to halt Lily with his words. 'You okay, Lily-Bee?'

'Dad, please.' His daughter shook her head as she turned to look at him, her tone acid. 'Just Lily is fine. I'm not five any more. I'm going to bed.'

He wasn't going to have an argument with an audience, so he acquiesced. 'Okay. I'll come up in a few minutes to say goodnight.'

'No need.'

'In a few minutes.' He tried to keep his voice level while also indicating to his daughter he would definitely be up to say goodnight. Like always. He could see the pain the photos had caused her, and he was going to make sure she was okay, whether she wanted him to or not.

She absentmindedly patted her pocket where she kept her phone. 'Can you make it a bit longer? Just got to double check my maths.'

He knew she was stretching the truth, but he let it go for the sake of keeping the peace.

Briana stood and picked the album up. 'Good-night, Lily.'

'Yeah.' His daughter nodded then disappeared upstairs again.

Bri's gaze followed Lily to the door and she said, 'Do you want to go up to her? Make sure she's okay?'

'I will in a little while. I've learned to leave her for a few minutes when she's upset or over-whelmed, otherwise she feels crowded.' He shrugged. 'There was a time when she'd come to me for comfort, not push me away.'

'She'll come back to you, Fraser.' Bri shot him a sympathetic look as she walked out into the hallway. 'I'm sorry if I've upset her.'

'Not at all. She looked like she was enjoying seeing pictures of her mum. It's not something we do enough of. Certainly not recently. With the help of the hospice Ellen wrote a little diary about her life and I know Lily treasures it, but it's lovely for someone else to tell her stories about her mum. And it's good for her to have an adult on her side other than me.' He hesitated, unsure where to go to from here. 'That is, if you're happy to be on her side?'

'That's what I signed up for, right? As a god-mother? I know I haven't been the best recently, but I want to make it up to her.'

He glanced upwards, imagining a grumpy Lily flopped on her bed. 'I can't promise it'll be easy.'

'I'm up for a challenge.' Briana flexed a bicep and laughed. His eyes were drawn to her mouth. Her lips were more sensual than he'd first noticed. Great mouth. Gorgeous eyes. Kind. Funny. She was the whole package.

He pulled open the front door and let her step in front of him out into the icy dark night. As she passed he got a whiff of her scent. Something fresh that reminded him of the little potted garden he'd tried to grow in London. Freesia or some sort of flower.

He was acutely aware of her. Feeling off balance by her being here. There was so much unsaid, so much anger and mistrust bubbling under the surface that they needed to deal with and yet there was an undercurrent of something else too…something he was trying hard not to notice.

The last thing Fraser wanted was to get involved in anything deeper with Briana—or any woman, for that matter, if he was going to be spending time with them. Like this. Mushing over photo albums, trying to make his daughter happy. Together. 'Thank you for bringing the photos. It was hard fought for, but you did get a smile.'

Bri turned to look up at him and beamed. 'More than once, so I'm happy with that. It's a start.'

'It is.' He had a sudden urge to run his thumb over that mouth. Followed by his tongue. He swallowed. *So inappropriate*. 'Right, then. I'll see you next week. Clinic.'

'Yes.' She blinked up at him and he was sure—as much as a man who hadn't dated properly since the beginning of the century could be sure—that there was a flash of heat in her eyes as she said, 'Oh, and we need to plan our sex—'

'Our what?' Heat rippled through him, singeing his nerve endings in a powerful sting of desire.

Whoa. It was unexpected, unbidden. Unwanted. What the hell was wrong with him?

'Sex education lessons.' Her eyes widened and her cheeks burned red. 'They're part of our contract. We give each year group age-appropriate sessions about boundaries, relationships and the developing body through puberty and beyond.'

Plan our sex. He couldn't get rid of an image of her lying on his bed, naked and satisfied. Or the wonder of what she would taste like. 'Oh. Yes. Of course. Do we…do it…' He swallowed again knowing he was making a total ass of himself. 'I mean…them…the lessons…together?'

'No. We split them up. We cover more ground that way.' Her lips twitched and eventually she laughed. More at him than with him he realised as she said, 'Fraser Moore, did you just think I was offering you sex?'

'Not at all. That would be ridiculous.' And yet…not so much. In fact, he took in her amazing body, long legs and perfect curves and thought it would be pretty damned stupendous.

Her expression changed from fun to confusion and then to rebuttal. 'Yes, it would. Don't you forget it.'

How could he? The thought of having sex with Briana had never entered his head for the whole time he'd known her.

But, right now, it was all he could think about.

CHAPTER FIVE

I MUST NOT think about Fraser's mouth.

I must not think about Fraser's mouth.

I must not...

Fraser's mouth. Perfect lips. Great teeth. Gorgeous smile. She'd been drawn to it. Watching him speak. And then...as they'd stood in the doorway, *wanting* that mouth on her.

It was happening all over again, despite everything. She'd wrestled her attraction to him under control years ago, or so she'd thought. There was no point wanting him. But, *man*, that mouth. His laugh. The sadness in his eyes that had twisted her heart.

A knock on the front door made her jump and had her heart slamming against her ribcage. *Tut-tut. Guilty minds.* 'Coming!'

Her ex-next-door neighbour and old friend, Beth, was standing on the doorstep of Bri's cottage in Lower Oakdale, her breath wisping out into the cool, crisp late-afternoon air as she spoke. 'Ready?'

'Totally.' Briana pulled on her trusty navy jacket, dragged on a matching bobble hat and locked the door behind her. 'I need a good walk and I'm so ready for a catch-up. It's been too long.'

'Like four years? More?' Beth grinned then glanced down at the leads in her hand that were starting to wind around her legs. 'I have a friend for you, if I can manage to untangle myself. Didn't want you to feel left out doing walkies without a dog.'

Ah. Bri looked at the large dog drooling onto her doorstep. There couldn't be many Old English sheepdogs around here. She bent down to ruffle his fur. 'Jasper?'

Beth frowned. 'You've met?'

'Indeed we have. He's messy, so watch out.'

'Tell me about it. But he's also adorable. I'm looking after him because his owners are busy.' Her friend sank her hand into Jasper's thick fur and then snuggled the other cute puppy bouncing up and down like the Energizer Bunny. One ear was floppy and the other stuck up to attention. He was just about the cutest thing Briana had ever seen. Beth laughed as he jumped and tried to lick her face. 'Okay. Okay. Don't be jealous. You have to share me. This is Boy. He's just learning how things are and he's a little excitable.'

'In that case, I'll take Jasper and make sure I keep my shoes out of drooling distance.' Bri took the Old English sheepdog's lead and fell into step with Beth.

Her friend grinned at her as they crunched through snow crystals that were turning to ice in the freezing dusk. 'Okay, spill the beans. I want to know everything about your Australia trip.'

Oh, no, you don't. 'Hot. Snakes. Spiders. Red dust.' She counted them off on her gloved fingers.

'Four years and that's all you've got to say?'

How to be honest about what had happened without telling the whole sordid, sorry story? 'Let's just say that going all that way with Tony wasn't my finest decision.'

'Why? I thought he was The One?'

'Er... No.'

Beth frowned. 'Did he break it off and break your heart too? Is that why you came home?'

'*I* broke it off. But far too late. To be honest, he wasn't the man I thought he was. He was...' The man she'd turned to when she'd been in despair over her friend's death, when she'd finally admitted her feelings for Fraser were completely one-sided. Briana took a deep breath and confided some of it to her friend. 'Turns out he was a bully. He felt he owned me, had a right to tell me what to do...'

Beth's eyes widened as she looked at Briana. 'I'm guessing that would not have gone down well.'

'It took a while for me to figure it out. He was

very subtle. But as soon as I extricated myself from him, I wanted to put as much distance between us as I could. So I came home.' Briana shivered and it wasn't all because of the icy temperature. 'Tell me about your love life, Beth. Mine's woeful.'

At that, her friend's mouth split into a wide grin and her eyes became sort of shiny and soft. 'I'm back with Alex.'

'That's a surprise.' The two of them had split up years ago.

As they trudged through Oakdale village Beth regaled her with the tale of their break-up and romantic Christmas reunion and Briana listened with envy. So far her own love life had been sadly depressing. There were lucky ones, she knew... people like Beth and Alex...but it just wasn't going to happen for her. She never wanted to risk her heart and her life again with a man. Never give anyone the chance to abuse and control her. And the thought of filtering through the bad ones just to find the possibility of a good one made her feel sick.

Beth sighed. 'I'm sorry things didn't work out with Tony. But you've been back here for months and we haven't seen you. Don't hide away. It's time to start over, right? You need to get yourself back out again, Bri.'

'I just don't know if I've got it in me to trust

a man again. Use them for sex, maybe.' She laughed and Beth did too.

'Atta girl. Scratch that itch.'

They were walking past Oakdale Medical Centre and she couldn't stop herself craning her neck to see if Fraser was there. Late Saturday afternoon? She didn't think so, but a girl could look, right?

Even if Fraser Moore was the last person she'd trust, he was definitely good eye candy.

And good at scratching an itch?

She was shocked that she'd even thought that.

The screechy whine of brakes had both women turning their heads. Caught in a slick of black ice, a car was descending the hill at speed. Directly towards them, and out of control.

There was barely a moment to think. Limestone wall behind them. House to left. Grass verge to right.

'Watch it!' Bri put her arm out and pushed her friend to the right, her heart thumping as her head whirred with dreadful possibilities. The dogs yelped. The car got faster. Closer. The yellow headlights pinned her against the wall.

This was it. This was the end. All breath stalled in Bri's lungs. She was frozen to the spot.

'Bri!' Beth shouted, as something tugged Briana sideways. Jasper? Beth? Ellen's ghost? Her dead friend was the last thing she thought of as she sprawled over the verge, hitting her head against the tarmac just as the car barrelled towards her, skimming her legs so closely she felt the shiver of air as it screamed past her into the wall with an almighty crash and grinding of metal.

She closed her eyes and let out a long sigh. She was alive.

Within moments there was a flurry of activity all round her. People came running out of their houses to investigate the noise. Bri sat up unsteadily, checking herself for damage then immediately thought about the people in the car.

The bonnet was concertinaed in a mess of bare metal. Smoke billowed from the grille at the front. An elderly lady sat in the driver's seat, looking stunned. She had blood dripping from a head wound but she was talking to Beth's boyfriend Alex and another doctor Bri knew from living around here, Joe Thompson.

And Fraser was there too—having materialised seemingly out of nowhere. He ran over to her. 'Bri? Are you okay?'

I am now. That was her first instinctive reaction. Swiftly followed by giving herself a very determined stern talking-to. She would not be okay just because a man was around. She would be okay because *she* decided she would be.

He knelt next to her and smiled. 'If you're going to have an accident, it's always best to do it near a medical clinic. Are you okay?'

'Go see to the people in the car. I'm fine.' She waved him away, noticing her hand was shaking.

'It's Mrs Wilkinson from the post office. She's a bit battered and bruised and definitely shocked but she's okay. Alex is there with Joe and Rose and they've called an ambulance as a precaution.' His eyes scanned her face and he gently pushed back her hair. 'I'm more concerned about you. You look pale. Anywhere else hurt?'

He was concerned about her. *First time ever.*

Her head was throbbing, but she was intact. At least physically. Although her body was prickling at Fraser's touch.

'I hit my head as I fell.' She patted down her body and her hand squelched against something wet and sticky on her jacket hem. She remembered being pulled down and thinking of Ellen. And if that wasn't enough to halt her soppy thoughts about Fraser, she didn't know what was. 'I think Jasper saved my life.'

'The Drool Meister does have his benefits after all.' Fraser smiled and just kept on looking at her. She couldn't drag her eyes away from his. It felt as if they were somehow connected, not physically but something else. On some other astral plane, or in other parallel life. That there was something bigger happening between them. Something important.

The knock to the head had clearly shaken something loose in there because she really, really wanted to slide into his arms and stay there yet he barely knew she existed. Not in *that* way anyway.

Beth wandered over and bent to look at Briana's head. 'Ouch. So, you two have met, then?'

'Weird story, but yes…we know each other from London.'

He stole my chance to spend the last two precious years of Ellen's life with her, she reminded herself before she got too carried away with his gooey eyes and gorgeous smile. With Fraser she'd started to let her guard down in ways she didn't want to allow.

'That looks nasty.' He pointed to her head.

'I'm fine.' She pressed her fingers to her forehead, and they came away damp. Red. 'I think I need to clean up a bit. My house isn't far away.'

'The medical centre's closer. Let's go there and I can have a proper look. It's too dark to see here. You might need stitches.'

No. Yes. No.

Before she knew it he was hauling her up, wrapping his arm around her waist as if she needed help walking and marching her up the road to the medical centre.

For fear of having a rerun of those silly flutters and longing glances that stoked an unwanted heat inside her, she refused to look him in the eye as he cleaned her wound. His closeness was unsettling. She liked the way he smelled of fresh snow mixed with the sharp tang of aftershave and something distinctly sexy. Liked the way he touched her with care and consideration, as if she was worth something.

Had Tony ever touched her like that? At first, yes. But things had changed. Things had changed between Ellen and Fraser too. Things always changed. And never for the better.

After he'd patched her up and washed his hands Fraser smiled. 'You look a lot more human now.'

'Urgh. What was I like before? Zombie, probably, with all that blood on my face.'

'Zombie? The least scary zombie I've ever seen.' The corners of his eyes crinkled as he laughed and she noticed tiny lines there. He'd had a rough few years. She imagined him dealing with a grief-stricken ten-year-old. Nursing a woman who wasn't his wife or lover through a devastating illness.

He put out his arm to help her up, but she shook her head, not wanting to be so close to him again. Not when her emotions were clearly all over the place. 'Thanks. I'm okay now. I'll head on home.'

'Everyone's gone to the pub. Fancy a drink?'

'Alcohol, with a head injury?' She shot him a cautious look.

'I meant just a lemonade or soda.' He slid his hand over hers, making her belly dissolve in a fizz of desire. 'I want to make sure you're okay. That was a nasty bump to the head.'

'I'm fine.' She tugged her hand away, shocked at the way her body yearned towards him. The way her insides melted into liquid at his touch.

Fraser Moore was not good for her resolve. But he was very good for her libido.

'Wait.' He reached out to double-check the cut on her head. Or so she thought. But he paused, fingertips on her temple, then they trailed down to her mouth. His thumb smudged across her lips, making her breath come fast and hard. Thoughts fuelled by pure desire swirled in her head. *Touch. Mouth. Taste. Kiss.*

He came closer. His breath warm on the side of her face. For a moment she thought he was going to kiss her. Wanted him to. Ached for that soft pressure of his lips on hers. His head tipped and he tilted her chin up, looking at her with such heat it made her tremble.

She swallowed, about to reiterate her refusal— because it would be the most foolish thing she could do—just as Beth breezed into the room, making them jump apart. 'There you both are! Alex has taken the dogs back to ours. Joe got us seats by the fire and there's a bottle of shiraz open. Come on.'

And so she wasn't allowed to refuse as her

friend grabbed one arm and Fraser took the other and they walked her round to the Queen's Head pub.

'You know, you can go home if you want. We're just concerned about you,' Fraser whispered a few minutes later as he brought her over a glass of lemonade then sat next to her. She was acutely aware of the press of his thigh against hers. Aware of the deep timbre of his laugh. The way his hand rested on his lap and the pleasure-pain longing for those fingers to slide over to her thigh. To feel them on her face again. To breathe him in. To kiss him.

She was going mad.

She edged away from him and from his heat. When he asked her a question, she tried hard not to look at him. Gave him one-word answers, anything not to spend more time under the gaze of those sexy eyes. Desperately searching for a distraction, she turned and spoke to the woman sitting across from her.

Rose had a healthy winter sun glow with white ski-goggle patches round her eyes. 'Apologies for the panda look.' She laughed. 'We got back from skiing yesterday. It was awesome. Bluebird skies every day. So, do you live in Oakdale?'

Bri nodded. 'I grew up next door to Beth and her mum. Then I went off to London to do my nursing training, stayed there for about ten years. Then did a stint overseas.' She wasn't going to go over that again, once was enough for today. 'Came back here in September.'

'I haven't seen you around.'

'I've been keeping a low profile.'

Rose nodded as if she understood. 'I'm glad Beth persuaded you to come for a drink. It's a lovely community here. Everyone knows each other and they've all been so helpful with our wedding preparations.'

'You're getting married? You and Joe?' Bri remembered Joe's first wife and the car crash that had killed her. She was glad he'd found happiness again. 'I'm so pleased for you.'

Rose smiled and looked the happiest Briana had seen anyone look in a long time. 'Ten weeks today and counting. I'm driving Joe mad with all the organising. The hen do is a month before. Oh!' She clapped her hands. 'You must come to the hen night. Please. Say yes.'

'Oh, no, I couldn't.'

'You'd be doing me a favour actually. Everyone knows Joe. His mum's bringing some of her friends and I'm going to be very outnumbered.' Rose winked conspiratorially. 'I'm looking for cavalry to be on my side and any friend of Beth's is definitely worth getting to know.'

Beth nudged Briana's ribs. 'Come on. It's a hen night. Booze, brides and bawdy games. What's not to like?'

It sounded fun and it had been a long time

since she'd had any. Bri breathed out and smiled. 'Okay, yes. I'd love to.'

'Give me your number.' Rose tapped the details into her phone. 'So, what prompted you to come back to Oakdale?'

I escaped and needed to find solace in the familiar.

'It's a beautiful place. When I saw the advert for the school nurse job, I just jumped at it.'

'Based where?'

'The team office is at Bowness Community Clinic. I cover a few primary schools across this area, but mainly I'm at the high school.'

'We run the adolescent outreach together,' Fraser interjected, and Bri's back stiffened at the sound of his voice oozing into the conversation. Along with it came the slam of lust she was trying hard to ignore. She turned her back to him. Swallowed deeply and tried to focus elsewhere.

Rose nodded. 'I think we're looking at that school for Katy when she's older. Oh, I don't want her to grow up, she's so lovely at eight. What's she going to be like at fifteen?'

'Yes, Fraser. Any tips for growing a good teenager?' Briana couldn't help throwing at Fraser.

I missed those lovely years because of you, she thought as a spark of anger mixed with the crazy desire inside her. *You stole my chance to be her friend. And now I can't get those years back. Precious moments. Lost. Because of you.*

And despite all that she wanted to kiss him.

So, it was official. She was all kinds of mixed up with him.

When she looked back at Rose the woman had a curious expression on her face.

'Let's just say that fifteen is…interesting. Give me eight any day,' Fraser said, collecting up the empty glasses. 'Anyone want another drink?'

At the cries of *yes* all round he looked at Bri. 'Fancy giving me a hand?'

The way he was looking at her and the tone of his voice gave her no option. 'Sure.'

When they reached the bar, he put the glassware down and turned to her. 'What's going on, Bri? You've either been ignoring me or throwing daggers at me all evening.'

'How's Lily?'

He blinked at the swift change in topic. 'She's much the same. Doesn't want to be here. Right now, she's babysitting Joe's daughter Katy.'

'That's good, right? Gets her out of the house.'

His jaw clenched. 'I much prefer it if I can see where she is.'

Her ire rose by a count of a thousand. 'You can't control her every move.'

'I'm keeping her safe.' He shook his head. 'I thought we'd been over this? I thought we were good?'

'We are far from good.' She couldn't help it. Even though she knew Fraser wasn't the type of

guy to do the things Tony had done—not at all—
just talking about her ex had resurrected all the
emotions, the fear and loneliness and panic. Not
to mention the reminder of her friend's death and
the anger she still had for Fraser about that. 'You
know, I'm not sure this move is working out for
you and your daughter. She's clearly miserable
and feels isolated. Why don't you just go back
to London?'

'Let's go outside.' Fraser touched her arm.
'Talk.'

'No!' she roared, just as the noise in the room
seemed to ebb. Eyes turned to look their way. She
shrugged out of his reach.

Even to her the things in her head didn't make
sense. How could she want to scream at him and
kiss him at the same time?

'Briana.' He glanced over to the table filled
with their friends and then back at her. 'Let's take
this outside. Please, before we become the main
act of the evening.'

Everyone was looking at them.

He was right, they had things to say and they
certainly didn't need an audience. She couldn't
live here and work with him and have this tumult
of emotions overwhelming her. Hell, it wouldn't
help her and it certainly wouldn't help her relationship with Lily. So, with words ready to tum-

ble from her mouth and her heart beating like an out-of-control train, she slid out the door and waited for him to follow.

CHAPTER SIX

FRASER STORMED ROUND to the side of the pub and called to her back, 'Okay, Bri. Let's have it out, once and for all. Get it out. Tell me what you think. Be honest. Don't hold back.'

Her chin tilted, haughtily. Her hands hit her hips. Primed to attack. 'I have nothing to say to you, Fraser Moore.'

'Yes, you do.'

Her eyes sparked hotly. 'Nothing polite, that is.'

'Just say it.' He prepared himself for a tongue-lashing and knew he deserved it. 'I hurt you. Right? You're furious with me and have been for years. You're also angry with yourself for not being the person you wanted to be for Lily. And you want to kiss me.'

Her eyes widened in rage. She blinked. 'I do not.'

'Two out of three isn't bad.' Interesting that she picked out the kiss on his list rather than the other things.

He was riling her on purpose, because if she

didn't say something now she'd keep it all bottled up, keep throwing daggers at him in front of their friends and they'd never move on.

But she did want to kiss him. He saw the heat in her eyes and knew it wasn't all anger. And he wanted to kiss her. Despite everything.

That was the weird thing. The angrier she got the more he wanted her. But they couldn't go on like this…flirting one minute, arguing the next. It was like being on a roller-coaster. He wanted to get off. But he also wanted to stay on for the wild ride.

Go figure.

She inhaled deeply. So did he. Because he didn't want more home truths thrown at him and he didn't want to relive what had happened five years ago, but it was as inevitable as his next breath.

'You should have let me see her.' Her eyes glittered as she glared at him. A look passed between them that made his skin tighten. An undeniable connection accepting there was anger and hurt and yet desire and need there too. It powered her words. 'I thought I'd done something wrong, hurt her in some way, and that was why she didn't answer my texts or calls. Why she sent messages through you. I used to stay awake for hours, staring into the dark, wondering what the hell I'd done to her. I thought… Actually, I didn't know *what* to think except that she must hate me for some reason.'

'She didn't hate you, Bri. She loved you.'

'Oh, yeah?' Her hands balled into fists. 'So why couldn't I see her? Why wouldn't you let me in? Let me know what was happening? I could have done more to help than leaving hot dinners on your doorstep and messages you rarely answered. I'm a nurse, Fraser, and I couldn't help my best friend. I could have cared for her. Something. Anything. Been her advocate. I just wanted to be there for her. So much. So badly.'

'She didn't want anyone apart from me and the medical team to see her like that. I tried to protect Lily from the worst of it.' And, honestly, he'd forgotten about the dinners… They'd magically appeared outside his front door and he'd heated them up and eaten them without thinking where they'd come from. He'd decided it had been a neighbour, or one of Lily's teachers, but it had been Briana. Trying to be involved. Caring. Loving her friend.

Now she was just angry. 'You were the gatekeeper between Ellen and the outside world, you could have let me in. Just for five bloody minutes. You could have fought for me.'

'And she would have hated me for it.' He imagined being in Bri's shoes and not being allowed to see a beloved friend. He would have fought this hard too. 'I didn't handle it well, I admit. But

I was doing what she asked me to do. It wasn't anything more than that.'

'It was *everything*.' She was so fired up, her expression animated. Magnificent. Brave. Loyal. 'I will never forgive you for not letting me spend the last dying months with my friend. Never.'

Gatekeeper. It sounded as if she thought he'd had more control over the situation than he'd had. 'I tried,' he growled. Wanting her to *hear* him. To listen. 'I reasoned with her. I begged her, for Lily's sake, if not for mine, to let other people in. But she made me promise. You don't think I wanted help? That I didn't want to share some of it with someone?'

'But she told me about the diagnosis when she first got it and we talked about it. We cried together.' Bri's bottom lip wobbled. 'Then she stopped answering my calls and it felt as if she just didn't want me around. I... I didn't understand.'

He hauled in oxygen as he relived those first unsure dreadful months of weird symptoms and diagnoses, then the horrific prognosis that had eventuated in two long years of battling. 'She was scared. She grew insular and had mood swings, forgetfulness, started lashing out. Headaches had her bedridden for days. Seizures exhausted her and made her zone out for hours afterwards. Her hair fell out in clumps.

'She couldn't bear to look at herself, never

mind anyone else look at her. I watched her fade right in front of me. She wanted to lock down at home with her unconventional family, insisting on keeping everyone else at bay. Trust me, I'd have given anything…*anything*…not to have to face all that on my own. Not to have to explain it to a nine-year-old. I would have given anything to have someone to talk to in those long dark nights when I was working out how to maintain a job and look after a child. I had to help my little girl through her grief while trying to work my way through mine.'

The words were rushing out of him like river rapids. Something about Briana's probing and pushing had cracked the dam he'd erected to protect himself. It was the most honest he'd ever been. And the most vulnerable. It was also the most he'd ever said to anyone about that painful, sad time.

'Now I'm here, trying to protect Lily all over again, and all you can do is hurl insults and insinuations at me as if I hurt you on purpose. As if I'm trying to punish my daughter. Who even thinks like that?'

She closed her eyes.

It hit him then. *Briana thinks like that. Why?* Someone else had hurt her. On purpose. His stomach felt as if it was in freefall and the only thing he wanted to do was haul her against his chest and hold her. And then find the person who

had made her think like this and lay into them.
With his fists. 'What happened, Bri?'

'This is not about me.' She turned away. 'This
is all on you.'

She would never listen. 'You know what? I'm
done here. It doesn't seem to matter how much
I say it, you won't accept it, but I didn't mean to
hurt you, Briana. I really didn't. It wasn't about
you, it was about Ellen. And Lily.'

He saw the way his words smacked into her
like bullets, the pain in her crumpled features as
he relived his bare existence of five years ago.
He wasn't going to bad-mouth decisions Ellen
had made in her final months, even if he hadn't
entirely agreed with them all.

He couldn't take it back. Couldn't pretend, either, that he'd coped, and managed just fine, the
way he'd told everyone at the funeral and in those
dreadful months afterwards.

He turned and walked away, unable to control
the fast rise and fall of his chest. He didn't want
her to see him scarred and raw, the same way
Ellen hadn't wanted anyone to see her so vulnerable. He got it. He understood. But Briana
didn't seem to.

She just wanted to make him pay. And he was.
Every day.

He crunched through the snow back towards
the pub, but felt a grab at his arm from behind.
When he turned around Briana was standing

there, eyes wide and huge, the cut on her head marring an otherwise beautiful face. Regardless of the fact he'd put an end to the conversation, she clearly hadn't finished with him yet.

'I'm sorry, Fraser. I was so angry at everyone and everything for such a long time and it's like you just turned on a tap and all the hurt came gushing out of me,' she said, her expression one of agony as she echoed the feeling he'd had—that once they'd started talking it had opened floodgates of emotion. That was why he generally preferred to keep his mouth shut on the subject of Ellen. 'I hate that you and Lily went through that. And I...well, I...' Briana's voice trailed off as she considered her next words.

He sensed her starting to hold back now. Unsure. Stepping into new ground. He saw in her the same tautness that bound his body, one of honour and duty and loyalty that meant he couldn't touch her hair or her skin or her mouth.

And, God, how he wanted to touch her mouth.

She inhaled deeply then sighed. 'Bloody cancer. And then...after...' Her lip wobbled. 'I was so angry and hurt I ran away to lick my own wounds instead of staying around and helping you with Lily when you needed me most. I just grabbed the lifeline that Tony offered and left. I was so raw and hurt so badly. And I feel so damned...' her eyes filled with tears '...*guilty* about it all. I should have been the godmother I promised to be. I should have stayed.'

'You have no reason to feel guilty, Bri. None at all. You did everything you could, everything that was asked of you, and you deserved to make choices about your life without taking anyone else into account. But I get it. The guilt. The helplessness. I'm a medic too. I should have had the answers, right? I'm sorry you were hurt. I really am. I should have said something sooner. Reached out. Something… But I didn't. I was busy with everything else. But I will not spend the rest of my life looking back at the mistakes I made. I refuse to be eaten up by the guilt or grief. I did what I thought was right at the time. I was looking after Ellen. And now I have to stay strong for Lily. And…'

He didn't want to sound selfish but, hell, sometimes you just needed to be. 'You know, for me too. I'm thirty-four, Bri. I have a lot of years left in me and I'm going to make them good ones. Ellen died five years ago and afterwards I tried to make a life. It didn't work out as I hoped so now I'm making another one.'

'I know how that feels. But a life without Ellen feels…less. I knew her for so long…a whole lot longer than you.'

'It's not a competition, Bri.' He felt his shoulders sag. 'Neither of us won. We both loved her. We both lost her.'

'I miss her.' She wrapped her arms round her chest. 'I don't know if I'll ever get used to her not being here. On the end of the phone, laughing at some silly story about Lily. Or something about you.' She gave him a wary smile then put her hand over his. Her eyes roamed his face and settled on his mouth. Embers of need flared into life. But the connection wasn't just physical, it was deeper than that. It was the weaving of needs and fears and vulnerability, it was a shared history—however complicated.

There was so much more he wanted to know about the last few years of her life. 'Tell me what happened to you.'

'No.' Her mouth flattened. 'Like you, I want to move forward. No point looking backwards for the rest of my life, right?'

'He hurt you.'

She nodded. 'He did.'

But she wasn't going to say any more, he could see. She took a long deep breath as if trying to find some equilibrium and he wasn't sure if it was because of his story or hers that she refused to tell, or the intense connection that had brought them to this point. Bearing their souls. The keeper of secrets.

He wasn't the keeper of hers. She didn't trust him enough to tell him what had happened.

Yet.

He made a promise to himself. Whatever happened, he wanted to be her friend at least, gain her trust so she could speak about her past without fear or the shame he saw in her eyes.

So maybe holding hands and spilling his guts wasn't the best move he'd ever made. Besides, he didn't do this. Didn't do relationships, because he didn't have time or space in his head for someone other than his daughter. Until recently, when all of his time and all of his headspace had been filled with Briana. And he definitely didn't do anything deeper than a fling, especially with someone who was going to stay around for Lily.

He swallowed as their gazes clashed. Pools of deep blue, honest and glittering and drawing him in deeper and deeper. Mesmerising him. 'Sounds like we both had a crappy few years.'

'Sure did. But now I'd like to help.' She squeezed his hand and ran her thumb across his palm.

He ignored the nerve-endings firing off pure lust as her cool skin smoothed over his. At least he tried to, but all he could think about was sliding his mouth over those perfect lips. It had been so damned long since he'd held a woman. So long he couldn't even remember. Seven years? Brief flings before Ellen had got sick and his life had become utterly focused on her and Lily.

He wanted Briana. He wanted to know what she tasted like, how she sounded when she came. He wanted to explore every inch of her. But what would happen then? He couldn't offer her anything. He didn't do relationships or commitment. He didn't have a blueprint for functional, only dysfunctional. 'I don't know, Bri. If every conversation is going to end up in a shouting match I don't think I can do it. I don't want to do it.'

'What if it ends like this?' She reached up and cupped his face. He registered her intention as need rippled through him. He tensed, holding back and back and back, but something deep inside him snapped.

It was the final crack, the dam breaking.

And, sure, there were a million reasons why they shouldn't take the next step, but he'd spent five years fighting and he was done with that. When her lips met his he groaned. His hands slid into her hair and he drew her closer, a gentle exploration at first, a learning of tastes and angles and shapes. The feel of her, her scent.

But it wasn't enough. He hauled her closer, wanting more of her. He wanted everything. And everything went into that kiss. All the anger and frustration and the out-of-nowhere need that invaded his thoughts and his dreams. She was the only person who knew what he'd been through and the way he felt.

The only woman he wanted right now.

She moaned as his tongue slipped into her mouth. He pulled her against him, relishing the feel of her in his arms, the sweet lemonade taste and the press of her soft body against his, unable to get enough of her.

He didn't want to question the sense of this, although his brain registered the complication. He shut it down. Maybe one kiss was all they'd need.

Yeah. He ran his palms down her back as he angled his mouth on hers, drunk on the taste of her. One kiss would never be enough.

And the flicker of a thought slid into his brain.

Maybe Briana was his fresh start.

CHAPTER SEVEN

'I WANT YOU,' Briana murmured into Fraser's mouth, shocked at the urgency she felt and the way his kiss made her want more. Want him everywhere. To scratch that itch that was getting harder to ignore or deny. The rage she'd felt before had exploded into wild, crazy desire, cracking open something carnal and base and freeing. He made her feel so angry, so flustered, so desperate. So damned hot.

He pulled her closer and she could feel how much he wanted her too.

'Briana—' He froze.

From somewhere in the darkness came voices, people laughing and chatting.

No. No. No. Don't stop.

She put a fingertip to his lips, making sure he didn't say a single thing that might make her change her mind. It had been so long since she'd taken control and taken what she wanted, and she was totally going to do this now. With Fraser.

How she'd wanted this all those years ago.

She'd put all those wishes in a box and closed the lid but now the box was open and she was going to take it all.

'My place. Closer…' She grabbed his hand and led him down narrow back streets, threading through the snowy village to her cottage, almost running in the rush to have him.

They barely made it through the door before his mouth was on hers again and he pressed her against the wall, covering her throat with delicious rough kisses that made her skin burn with pleasure. He tugged off her coat and threw her hat on the floor then stepped away just for a moment to look at her.

'God, Briana you are amazing. This is all I've been thinking about doing for days.' He slid his mouth over hers, his kiss hot and greedy as his hand cupped her buttocks. He pulled her closer. Their gasps came faster and harder, greedy to taste and explore each other. He palmed her breast over her clothes. There was too much fabric between them. She wanted him naked, to slide her skin against his.

'Upstairs…' she managed on a desperate breath, then she was pulling him up to her bedroom.

The moment she closed her bedroom door he pulled off her jumper and T-shirt in one swift move then laid her on the bed. In the soft glow of a sidelight she could see his beautiful face, the need in his eyes that fuelled hers.

'Do you think they're all still waiting for their drinks?' He laughed as he reached round and unclipped her bra then ran feathery strokes across her nipples that made her curl into him, wanting his mouth there too.

'I'm sure they can manage to sort themselves out.' She snatched wet kisses in between shucking off his layers of clothes. Winter clothes were too thick and cumbersome and took too much time to come off. As she flicked his T-shirt to the carpet she took in the dips and planes of his body. God knew when the man had time to work out but it was clear he did. She ran her palms over the hard, defined pec muscles. 'Meanwhile, I want you to sort me out, Fraser Moore.'

This man who'd cracked her resolve by pushing her. By expecting her to be honest and nothing less. Who had stood there and taken her truth and not belittled it. He'd explained what had happened and why. But he hadn't told her she was being ridiculous, that she was whining, that she didn't deserve to feel like that.

This man who she'd shouted at in a way she'd never spoken to anyone before. Who had then apologised for what he'd done when he'd been going through the worst thing anyone could have to endure. And he was still fighting, for his daughter if not for himself, making changes and choices that were difficult but right. Despite what Bri had assumed to the contrary.

Now the only thing she wanted was to feel his arms around her. To feel his heat.

'I'm going to have some serious explaining to do tomorrow.' He palmed her breast, rubbing and stroking until she thought she would lose control completely, then his mouth found her nipple and he sucked it in.

'Oh, my God. That feels so good.' She writhed against him. 'Don't you dare explain this.' She laughed as she tugged down the zipper on his jeans and palmed his erection. *Oh, man.* 'Let's get you out of these.'

'My pleasure.' He laughed as their arms tangled in the rush to relieve him of his jeans and boxers.

Oh, man.

She took hold of him and stroked. He was so hard and so big and she wanted—ached—so much for him. He took her hand away and placed both her arms above her head, pinning her on the bed, then straddled her. 'I want to kiss you everywhere.'

She couldn't move.

Unwelcome memories rushed into her head. *'Stay there. Do not move until I say so.'*

Panic wove through her. She took a breath, opened her eyes, forcing herself to look at him.

It's Fraser. It's okay. It's Fraser.

It's Fraser...finally.

But suddenly feeling vulnerable, and not wanting to feel like that ever again, she snatched her hands back, her heart thrumming hard against her ribcage. 'Let go. Now. Let me go.'

His body went completely still, his expression shocked and confused. He rubbed his forehead as he rocked backwards away from her. 'Geez, Bri. I'm sorry. I thought you wanted—'

'It's...' She willed her heart rate to slow. Battled the unease that stemmed from her past and not from this man.

Sex Ed for Beginners. Be honest about your boundaries. Tell him what you want and don't want. Be in control of your own body.

'You thought right, Fraser.' Saying his name anchored her. She was here in her bed with a gorgeous man. A man who wanted her, liked her, respected her. 'I asked you here. I want you here. I just don't like being held down.'

He stroked her cheek with the backs of his fingers. 'No. Of course. I'm sorry, I was just playing.'

'I know.' She closed her eyes, expecting him to ask her for more details. Expecting him to leave.

But he didn't. He lay down next to her and wrapped his arms around her, spooning her and whispering against her neck, 'Whatever you want. Or don't want. I'm okay with it, Bri.'

She closed her eyes, glad he couldn't see the

flush rising on her face. Being honest was harder than she'd expected. 'I don't like feeling trapped, that's all. I want to do this, Fraser. Honestly, more than anything. You're incredible. But I like... being in control.'

'Now, that I can work with.' She felt his grin against her neck.

'Don't get the wrong message here, big guy.' She chuckled. 'I just mean I don't like being out of control. No holding me down.'

'I get it. I think.' He stroked down to her hip-bone and turned her to face him, all serious and genuinely concerned. 'Your pace. Your call.'

Her heart squeezed at his gentleness and she took his hand and ran her tongue along his palm. She watched as he squirmed, closing his eyes as his breathing quickened again. 'I call for more kisses. Then...' she made sure she captured his gaze '...we'll see where that takes us.'

'To wherever you want to go, Briana.' He cupped her face and kissed her so gently, so thoroughly and for so long that her momentary fear became a dim memory. She lost herself in his caresses, the gentle exploration of his fingers, in his exquisite taste.

She forgot everything except his touch, his next kiss. Wherever he stroked her skin she wanted his mouth there too. She learned what made him flinch with desire as she brushed her fingertips down his belly. Learned the feel of him, the shape of him, the dips and valleys of his body. The tight, well-honed muscles. Learned he'd take things at her pace, but that her pace suddenly wasn't fast enough for even her and that she wanted him the way she'd never wanted a man before. Learned also that he truly did want to give her pleasure and not just take it for himself.

Learned that what she said, he would do and that gave her courage.

So when he asked, 'What do you want?' she laughed. And then told him.

'I want you to kiss me all over.'

'Mind-reader.' He sucked in her nipple, sending shivers of anticipation and pleasure through her. 'Lucky me.'

She lay there, almost completely naked and, okay, feeling just a little bit vulnerable but knowing she was completely safe and very turned on—and she knew that didn't make sense. But where Fraser was concerned none of her reactions made sense.

By all accounts she hated him.

But he made her feel so utterly sexy and wanted. It was a battle of emotions and a battle of wills. And right now she felt as if she was winning. She was utterly in control and wanting so very desperately to scratch that itch Beth had talked about.

Beth. Sitting in the pub with the others, waiting for another drink.

Briana giggled.

Fraser slicked kisses down her abdomen, wriggled off her panties and then slid his hand between her thighs. His fingers found her centre and she arched, moaning with pleasure as he seemed to instinctively know what she wanted, the right pressure, the right rhythm.

Then his mouth was on her and her fingers were in his hair. As he kissed her most intimate places she felt wound up tighter and tighter until she could barely think. She gave herself up to the sensations, to him. Desperate. Wanting. Needing. 'Oh, God. Fraser. Don't stop. Don't…'

Then she spiralled out and up and into a million pieces, slumping back against the pillows, her body rippling and yet wanting more. Wanting all of him.

'Fraser.' She barely recognised her own voice it was so thick with sex. 'That was amazing.'

'You think we've finished?' He kissed his way back up, taking a long and delicious detour over her breasts. She was grateful he wasn't asking her permission or waiting for her say-so because she couldn't think past wanting him inside her, never mind find words to actually voice it.

His erection pressed against her thigh, still hard. Harder. She took him in her hands and stroked. Fraser's eyes fluttered closed on a sharp inhalation. 'This is not going to be so memorable if you keep doing that. Or maybe memorable for all the wrong reasons.' He laughed then kissed her hard, pressing her into the duvet. Her back against soft linen, her front pressed hard against solid muscle.

She stroked him faster. He stayed her hand.

'I need to be inside you.' His voice was halting and as desperate as she felt. 'Condom?'

'I'm a sex educator. Of course I have condoms.' She reached out and dragged her work bag across the floor and grinned as she offered it to him.

His eyes grew wild as he looked at the hundreds of condoms in there. Different coloured packets, ribbed, flavoured. So much choice.

'So many?' His eyes danced with laughter and surprise.

'Be prepared, right? That's what I teach them.'

He peered inside the bag again. 'Um. Do you have a preference?'

You. She giggled. 'Do a lucky dip.'

He laughed as he plunged his hand into the bag and brought out a random foil packet. 'Ah. So we have ribs and dots…' He squinted. 'For added pleasure and sensation. Lucky me.'

She smiled and reached to pull his mouth to hers. 'Lucky me.'

He ripped open the foil and sheathed, his smile fun and yet serious. 'I am so glad you decided to rage at me in the pub car park.'

'So am I.' Her voice was husky and cracked, the way she felt with him. Cracked open and raw and sexy and wanted. She'd reached up and kissed him, tired of the push and pull, wanting to take action. Finally. Taking something for herself.

Things got serious then as he gazed at her as if he could see everything she wanted, everything she was thinking and feeling. And as if he understood, accepted her for who she was and who she wanted to be.

He ran his thumb over her top lip. 'Are you sure about this?'

'More than anything. But, wait…' She edged out from underneath him and pushed him back on the bed. Then she climbed onto him, straddling him. Taking his erection into her hand, positioning it at her entrance. 'That's so much better—'

Her words caught at the tight press as she lowered herself over him. Shocked at how he filled her, the pleasure-pain thrill. The thrill too of watching his face—the pure ecstasy in his features, the tremble in his limbs. Knowing she made him feel so good. Knowing she was in control. Taking this for herself. One night with Fraser.

'Oh, God.' He gripped her hips as she picked up a rhythm. His eyes fixed on hers as he thrust and she rode, a sexy smile on his lips as he leaned up and snaked his hands into her hair and pulled her to him. 'You are amazing, Briana. Tell me what you want.'

'This. You. All of it.' She wanted all of him. Skin to skin. Lips to lips. Pressing all of her against the length of him.

He flipped her onto her back and thrust deeper into her, his fingers sliding between where they joined. And still he looked at her as if she was the only woman on earth. His mouth found hers and he kissed her with a reverence she'd never experienced before and could only lose herself in. Then his rhythm quickened and the kiss became a desperate, greedy clash of teeth and spit and moans. She bucked against his hand, a delicious tension spiralling once again inside her.

He groaned her name, thrusting harder and faster and took her with him, sensation after sensation rippling through her, in her, over her. And she didn't ever want it to stop.

It took Fraser more than a few minutes to come back to reality.

He was in bed with Briana. Not sweet eighteen-year-old Briana all excited about moving to London with her best friend. Not angry Briana who hated him, or his daughter's godmother, or Ellen's best friend.

This Briana was more complex, more nuanced. Someone who'd lived through darkness—although she wasn't ready to tell him about it yet. Someone who was unbelievably sexy and sensual.

It had been damned fine sex and his head was still adjusting. His body was still in *wanting* her mode.

But…what now?

He hadn't thought past having her. Hadn't thought at all, just touched and kissed and rubbed and… God, it had been good.

But…what now?

Her blonde hair was fanned out on the pillow, the soft glow of the sidelight illuminating perfect skin, hooded post-sex eyes. A very sexy smile. His heart clenched to look at her. Not just because he knew it had been a mistake but because he didn't want it to be one.

He stroked her thigh. 'Well, that was unexpected.'

'I don't…can't remember doing anything like that before…so…*desperate*…' She laughed. 'Ever.'

He settled next to her, propped himself up on his elbow, his chin in his palm, already aching to be inside her again and knowing that would definitely be a mistake. 'How long is it since you had sex?'

She shrugged a shoulder and laughed. 'Too long. You?'

'Same.'

She rolled onto her side to face him and ran her finger across his collarbone. 'Have you dated much since Ellen?'

'The odd fling before she got sick. Pretty hard to do anything more than temporary when you're dealing with all that. Then they both moved in with me full time and that completely put a stop to any kind of anything.' His eyes shuttered closed briefly as he pushed back the memories. 'I haven't had a serious girlfriend since Ellen. Lily wouldn't cope with someone else in my life and I have to put her first.'

'So...' Bri's smile dipped. 'That's...definitely a reason not to do this again.' She paused, her eyes roaming his face, searching for something. He didn't know if she'd found it when she said, 'Right? This isn't going to happen again.'

He hadn't been expecting that. He tried to read her. Tried to work out what this feeling in his chest was. Was she willing to just walk away after this? Was he?

He put some light into his voice. 'Are you regretting this already, Briana?'

'No. Not regret.' She bit her lip. 'It was good, very good.'

'But life's complicated enough, right?' He jumped in.

He wasn't sure what he saw flickering across those beautiful features, but she nodded. 'Something like that.'

He felt a need to explain. 'It's hard enough, just the two of us. Adding someone else into the mix would be chaos. To be honest, I've had enough chaos to last me a lifetime.' Was it unfair to put all the emphasis on Lily? When he had a feeling that his reluctance about having a relationship boiled down to the fact he didn't want to invest emotions in someone who might leave. Or stamp on his heart the way his father had done to his mother. The way his mother had done to him. Even Ellen had left him. Why put your heart on the line only to be left hurting at the end?

Bri ran fingertips over his collarbone. 'I'd hope I wouldn't be the chaos-maker, in another parallel world where we did decide to do this again. But it's okay. I understand. I don't need a relationship either, but I hope you'll still let me see Lily. I want to get through to her. Be there for her.'

'Of course.' He kissed her, because he couldn't not. And who knew when he'd ever do it again? He wanted this to count, to remember it. For her to remember him. 'We can't let this…what happened be a barrier to working well together or to your relationship with Lily.' He smoothed her hair back from her face, smudged his thumb across her cheek.

'Good. Thank you.'

'There's more, though. Isn't there?' He'd felt the tension slide back into her.

'I just don't want a relationship right now. I've not long got out of a difficult one.'

'Difficult how?'

'Enough to put me off relationships for a long

time. He did things, said things that rocked me. It's taken me some time to work through all of that. Hence the wobble I had.'

Shame rippled through him. 'I would never hurt you, Bri. Never.'

'I know. At least, you'd try not to.' She smiled and something in his gut uncurled. 'And the surprise of it all is that, despite what I've been thinking, you are a good man, Fraser Moore.'

He laughed. 'If you talk to Lily you might believe something different.'

'She's struggling to find her way too. Just make sure you teach her her worth and to speak up for herself any time she feels uncomfortable.'

'Trust me, my daughter is not one to hesitate about speaking up.'

'I wish I'd grown up like that. Might have saved me a bit of heartache.'

Which of course made him want to know so much more than she was telling him. 'I know I'm not supposed to ask questions, Bri. So I won't. It's your past and it's private. But if you ever want to talk about it, I'm here.'

'Thanks.' She put her hand over his heart. 'I know.'

'Not every guy is the same as him. Some of us are actually okay.'

'You're more than okay, Fraser.' She slid out of the sheets and he got the message it was time for him to leave.

He reached for his discarded clothes and dressed almost as quickly as she'd undressed him and with a lot less excitement. 'From now on we'll stay firmly in the friend zone. I promise I won't venture out of that box again.'

She slipped her arms into a silk kimono-style robe, tied it across her waist and settled back onto the bed. 'Friend zone? Okay. Yes. I can do that.'

Until an hour ago they'd been close to enemies. Someone to mistrust. Someone to blame. Someone to have damned fine sex with. And now he was just plain confused.

She was quite serious. 'It's probably best if we don't see each other outside work. At least not in the short term.'

'When Lily's your goddaughter? How's that going to work?'

'I'll arrange to see her away from you. Girl time, you know? I bet she'd be glad for some of that.'

'Good plan.' It should have felt like a lucky escape from what might have been a complicated scenario. She was making it so easy for him to walk away, but he had a strange tight feeling in his chest.

He sat opposite her and despite what they'd just agreed he wanted to take his clothes off, slip his hands underneath that silk robe and stroke her skin. To kiss her again and more. To hear her story. Maybe spend the night... Yeah, definitely parallel universe wishing. Instead, he was forcing himself to build the barriers back up. She was off limits. They both knew it was the right thing to do. He patted his pockets to locate his phone. 'Any idea what time it is?'

'Ten fifty-three.'

'What?' He jerked up. 'I've got to get back.'

'Lily?'

'Of course Lily. Always Lily.'

The smile had gone but she put her hands on his chest and pushed. 'Go.'

But he grabbed her hand and kissed the knuckles. 'Thanks, Bri.'

'Hey, big guy, I scratched an itch.' She winked. 'The thanks are all mine.'

CHAPTER EIGHT

Six weeks later...

TWO BLUE LINES.

Bri sat on the loo and stared at the white plastic stick in her hand. Her mouth went dry and her throat felt raw. Tears pricked at her eyes, but she blinked them back. She was not going to cry over this.

Oh, God.

Pregnant.

Not that she was surprised. Her period was late, her boobs were sore. She knew the signs. She was a medical professional after all. She knew that condoms weren't one hundred percent effective. That was what she told her students. Every. Single. Day.

She wafted her hand in front of her eyes to dry the mascara that was getting decidedly runny. Why had she decided to do this right before the hen night?

Another stupid decision. But she'd been too

cowardly to do the test earlier, preferring to live in wilful ignorance and not face up to the truth, but then Beth had turned up with a bottle of wine and Briana had panicked. Should she drink alcohol? Could she be…?

Yes, she was.

Pregnant.

This hadn't been part of her plan. What the hell was she going to do?

She sniffed as a tear ran down her cheek. Okay, maybe she was going to cry. Just a little bit.

'Hey! Bri!' Beth hammered on the bathroom door. 'The minibus is going to be here in a few minutes, and I need to use the loo before we leave.'

Damn.

'I'm just finishing up.' Bri fisted away the rogue tears. She took a deep breath. Then another. Then she slid the test back into its box, stuffed it into the cupboard under her sink and washed her hands.

How was she going to explain away why she wasn't touching alcohol on a hen night? Headache? Antibiotics? Yes. She rifled through her medicine cabinet and found a tub of old flucloxacillin capsules and stuffed it into her handbag as proof, in case anyone asked. Because she sure as hell couldn't tell them she was pregnant before she'd had time to think about what she was going to do. Or before she told Fraser… The thought of that made her feel nauseous.

After their amazing sex she'd watched him retreat emotionally. Seen the relief when she'd casually suggested they not do it again. She'd been so confused about the way she was feeling…scared even by how *much* she was feeling. Losing herself.

Neither of them wanted a baby right now. Hell, she'd never even thought about having a baby… that was what grown-up, organised people in a relationship did. The thought was terrifying.

Another knock on the door, this time more urgent. 'Bri! Please. I'm bursting.'

'Okay. Sorry.'

Another deep breath. *Glad rags on, game face primed.* She ran her finger under her eyes then looked in the mirror at the black trails down her cheeks. *Ugh.*

'Just tarting up the mascara. One minute.'

She threw the door open and Beth gasped. 'Wow. You look amazing.' She stuffed something soft and silky into Bri's open hand. 'Put this on. Quick!'

It was a white sash with the words *Team Bride* inked in glittery silver letters. Bri sagged a little inside but slid the sash over her head, wishing with all of her heart that she could rewind her life. Back to when?

Before sex with Fraser?

Saying yes to the hen party invitation?

Returning to Oakdale?

Before Tony?

She shivered. *Well, girl, you can certainly pick them.*

Fraser and Tony were worlds apart, chalk and cheese in looks and personalities. But neither were suitable. Neither was right for her. One was too much of a bully. The other was too…everything.

Pregnant.

Be careful what you wish for.

She'd had her one time with Fraser but what the hell would he say now? She put her hand to her belly and felt panic ripple through her. The last few weeks had been difficult. Despite what they'd agreed, the sex had loomed between them. Awkward didn't come close to explaining it.

Lily had been elusive. Always busy when Briana suggested coffees or catch-ups. Not interested in girl time…or at least not girl time with Briana. Her goddaughter was a hard nut to crack and Bri hoped it wasn't too late to fix things between them.

And now she was expecting Fraser's child.

She thought of the girls who came to her clinic and the options she talked through with them. The leaflets she gave them, the phone calls she made. But they were teenagers and she was a grown-up. She had the wherewithal to take care of herself and anyone else who came along.

She was strong—terrified, but strong.

'Hey, daydreamer, you okay?' A grinning Beth grabbed her arm and tugged her towards the front door.

'Sorry. Yes. I was miles away. I'm fine.'

Far from fine. Very far.

Pregnant.

She thought of Lily and the lost girl she'd become. Of Fraser's words… *'My daughter comes first. Life's complicated enough. I've had enough chaos to last me a lifetime.'*

Would he even want to be involved? What the hell was she going to do?

A honk outside had Beth running to the door. 'Right. It's here. Come on, Briana. For goodness' sake, smile! This is where the fun starts!'

Bri heard the minibus before she saw it. Raucous laughter, giggles and loud pumping music. Fun? Maybe for the rest of Team Bride. But Briana couldn't wait for the day to end.

Fraser hadn't realised he'd been looking out for her until he saw her across the crowded pub and he instantly relaxed and perked up at the same time.

She was with the hen party, all laughing and drinking, taking up most of the back half of the room. As the stag group wandered over, the noise intensified with shrieks of both delight and horror at the two groups meeting.

In the middle of the chaos Briana lifted her head and caught his eye, held his gaze for a moment and then abruptly turned away.

Pretty much the way things had been going for the last few weeks. Conversation had been tense. Not worse than before, but different. Trying to work alongside her had driven him to distraction—half because he wanted to kiss her, half because he didn't know how to act around her.

At least when they'd been angry with each other he'd known how to feel. Now everything was muddied. His body prickled with need every time he looked at her. He couldn't get the image of her naked body out of his head every time he looked at her. Couldn't forget the way she tasted, the soft moans. Working out a teaching programme with her on sex education had been... interesting.

His mind may have decided one thing, but his body had another idea altogether.

Time to clear the air.

Again.

He sauntered over, trying to ignore the catch in his chest as he took in her tousled hair, the short black dress that hugged her body and the high-heeled shoes that matched the silver writing on her sash. She was radiant as she laughed at something Rose said to her but there was something different about her too, a light in her eyes, a softness he'd never noticed before. It suited her. He had to shout be heard over the loud music and chatter. 'Hey, Bri. This is weird, right? The hen and stag meeting up in the same pub?'

'It was bound to happen.' She shrugged, the softness replaced by something that made her untouchable and the light in her eyes extinguished by increments the closer he got to her. 'Kendal's a small place.'

'Having fun?'

'Great. Yes. Fun.' Not smiling, she lifted her glass and drained it. 'Cheers.'

Okay. 'You want another drink?'

'I'm fine, thanks. We're going soon. A pub crawl isn't a crawl if we stay in one place.'

There it was. The guardedness she'd worn since the night they'd had sex. Whether it was the booze or he'd reached the end of his tether he wasn't sure, but something made him speak up. 'Look, what's going on? There's a weird vibe, right?'

'I don't know what you mean.' She blinked quickly. 'How's Lily?'

That came out of left field, but he was glad she'd asked. 'Not great, to be honest. I think you were right the other day when you told me to go back to London. She's not settling here. She's not happy.'

'But... I thought...' Bri's eyes widened. Then

she nodded and her arm curled protectively across her belly, like a barrier. 'I see. Right. Okay.'

'I mean…nothing's planned or anything. But I hate seeing her like this. She's all I've got, you know? Maybe I did the wrong thing by moving her up here.'

Bri pressed her lips together. The colour had drained from her face. 'But London? It's so far away.'

And yet you told me to go.

'Look, Bri, I think we need to talk.'

Her eyes filled and she blinked quickly.

His stomach clenched and he suddenly felt the most sober he'd been his whole life. Was she about to cry? 'What's wrong, Bri? What's the matter?'

Her expression flattened and she shook her head. 'Nothing.'

'Yes, there is. What is it?' Was it because he'd said he'd considered moving back to London? But then…she'd made it clear she didn't want anything more. He had a sudden unpleasant thought. 'He's not back, is he?'

She frowned. 'Who?'

'The guy. The one who hurt you.' His hands curled into fists in an unbidden and instinctive act of protection. He shook them loose before she called him out on being a Neanderthal.

'Tony? I hope not.' Her back stiffened and she

walked him away from the rest of the group. 'What do you know about that?'

'Only what you told me.' *Or didn't tell me.* 'I've been thinking about it.'

'Well, don't.'

It wasn't as if he was going to forget the look on her face as he'd held her arms above her head. 'If it's not him, what is it?'

'Please, Fraser. Shut up. This is not the place to have this conversation.'

His heart thudded. What did she mean? 'What conversation?'

Her eyes fluttered closed. 'Nothing. Look—'

What conversation? What was wrong? What had happened?

'Can I call you? Tomorrow? Morning?'

A swaying Beth was tugging on Briana's arm. 'Come on, chatterbox. We have more pubs to go to and more games to play.'

'Okay.' Bri shot him a look then grinned at her friend. Only someone who knew her as well as he did, someone who'd seen beyond her guard, would know she was digging very deep to find that smile. 'Right, then…what's next on Rose's dare list?'

Beth squinted at a piece of paper in her hand. 'Um… She's kissed a bald man's head, so now she has to…oh, yes. Drink a shot without using her hands.'

'Okay. Let's go.'

Bri didn't even turn back to look at him. She just swished out of the bar with the rest of the women, leaving him with a rather drunk Joe who was trying to throw a dart at the dart board and missing not just the outer rings but the whole board altogether.

Fraser looked back at the door swinging on its hinges and wondered what the hell had got Briana so riled up.

She could be damned well sure he was going to talk to her tomorrow.

Tomorrow came far too quickly in the form of a knock on her door at five-thirteen a.m.

Before she even answered, Briana knew who it was going to be. But, far from the drunken mess she was expecting, he looked very sober indeed.

He was still wearing his smart shirt and chinos from last night under his thick coat. His hair was damp, his nose and the tips of his ears were red from the cold, but he looked just about as gorgeous as she'd ever seen him.

Her heart lifted and melted a little at his wary smile. Which made everything feel worse. 'Fraser. You said you'd call me in the morning.'

'It's morning now. I've been walking around the village for two hours, trying to work out what it is you need to talk to me about. And none of what I've conjured up in my head is good. You said your guy wasn't back, so are you sick?'

'What? No. What made you think that?' Then the penny dropped. He'd nursed Ellen, so of course his thoughts might go straight to that.

He nodded, obviously relieved, but his face was still pale as he walked into her hallway and closed the door against the icy blast whipping round their legs. He followed her into the kitchen where she flicked the kettle on, popped teabags into two mugs and tried to find the right words to say.

But he beat her to it.

'So you're pregnant, then?' he said in a tone that suggested he was joking and that he very much hoped she wasn't.

'Yes.'

His eyes closed and he sighed out a long breath. He looked as if this was the worst possible news he could ever receive. Her heart crumpled in on itself.

'Okay.' He ran his hand over his hair. Opened his eyes. And she saw a struggle there. Confusion. A little panic and yet something fiercely protective. 'Condom failure?'

'It happens. Should have picked a different one, eh?' She wished she'd stayed on the Pill after Tony. Wished Fraser had picked the strawberry- or chocolate-flavoured one. Any of the hundreds in that bag except the one he'd fished out.

But she didn't wish she'd never had sex with

Fraser because that brief happiness had been wonderful.

'So much for lucky dip. And you're going to keep it? Or...?' He swallowed. 'Only I know it's your decision and I'll support whatever that is. But, for the record, I'd look after you both, financially, obviously. And...whatever else you need.'

It occurred to her that this was a rerun of his past. *Déjà vu.*

He hadn't loved Ellen, although they'd briefly been smitten in that intense hot flash of young infatuation that was doomed never to last. But they'd worked out a co-parenting schedule and he'd supported the mother of his child and taken good care of Lily.

But this was different. At least, it was for Briana.

She sighed. 'I haven't really thought past the fact I had some blue lines on a stick yesterday. But, yes, I'm going to keep it.' She knew without a shadow of a doubt that she was going to love and protect this child growing inside her, regardless of what Fraser Moore wanted. 'I know this isn't what you want or need.'

'It's done, Briana. It's not as if I haven't been here before. You'd think I'd have learned the first time.'

There wasn't a flicker of emotion in his face now he was processing it. No congratulations. No *Isn't this wonderful. Our baby.*

'But I never had a dad around and I always swore I'd do everything I could for my kids if I ever had any. And now look… I have two. Give me a little time to talk to Lily. It's not been easy the last few weeks. She's refusing to talk to me because I won't let her go to London for next week's half-term.'

'Are you still thinking of moving back there?' Why had she put that thought in his head? She'd been so angry and frustrated and guilty, and wanting him…awash with out-of-control emotions but long-distance parenting would be so hard.

He scuffed his hand through his hair. 'I don't know, Bri. I feel as if the ground keeps shifting under my feet just as things get onto an even keel.'

'I've only just had a positive pregnancy test, Fraser. We both know anything could happen from here. We can wait until twelve weeks before we say anything to anyone. Should probably wait, actually. No point in upsetting Lily or rashly changing plans if nothing comes of it.'

'I don't like keeping secrets from her, but I can wait until we're sure.' His eyes dipped to her belly. 'Tell me what you need. I'd like to come to the scans.'

'Of course. I'll let you know as soon as I book one.' It was all going too fast. She hadn't the space or time or inclination to be a mother. But here she was.

It wasn't exactly what she'd wanted. It was a shock. But they'd have to live with it. And somehow work it out together.

Apart.

CHAPTER NINE

THREE DAYS INTO half-term and Fraser's blood pressure was spiralling out of control.

Briana's bombshell news had knocked him completely sideways.

How were they going to navigate this? Especially if he went back to London.

A baby changed everything.

It felt as if he was living in a Groundhog Day of his own making.

The biggest difference between this time and the last was that he'd had no long-term spark with Ellen. Hadn't had that ache in his chest when he looked at her—sure, he'd loved her as a friend, but he hadn't had that *can't stop thinking about you* craving like he had with Briana.

He'd have to wrangle the craving under control. He'd have to focus on the baby and not on the mother. On the practicalities of the situation and not on the way Bri brought out emotions in him that he wanted to hide from.

He glanced around his kitchen, imagining the

highchair stage all over again and realising he'd have to baby-proof it. Just as he'd seen the light at the end of a particularly challenging child-rearing tunnel.

And teenagers should come with a government health warning, he mused as he cleared up the kitchen after last night's dinner. Lily's job. Not done before she'd headed off to babysit Katy up the road and he'd gone to the Ambleside climbing wall with Alex.

He looked at the dog bowls on the floor. Empty. Jasper hadn't been fed. Also Lily's job, and a condition of getting the pet in the first place. As he walked to the dog food cupboard Jasper wound through his legs, almost tripping him up.

'Watch it, mate.' Fraser slopped food and water into the bowls. 'Thank your lucky stars you don't have to worry about anyone but yourself, Jasper, my boy. It's a dog's life all right. Sometimes I really, *really* want to be you.'

As he straightened up his phone pinged with a text message from Briana.

All okay for the scan this afternoon? Should I meet you there? Penrith Maternity Hospital. Two o'clock.

A sharp stab of pain slid under his ribcage. The kind of pain that was bound up with love and protection and a solemn promise. Briana had pulled strings and got an early gestation scan at the maternity unit. Not routine, but she'd wanted to double-check everything was fine and he'd agreed.

Keeping his distance was probably in order, but nothing would stop him going to this scan. Not even the flash of heat at the thought of spending time with Miss Off Limits.

He sent a message back.

I'll be there.

Now all he had to do was find an excuse to tell Lily about where he was spending the afternoon. So much for always being honest. But he'd promised Bri he'd wait before he said anything about the baby to his daughter, so he'd wait. Already things were getting more complicated.

Somehow, he'd managed to get through the last days of his half-term break on autopilot, cooking, hiking the hills around their village with Lily, trying to distract her from her never-ending pleas to go to London and hoping she'd fall in love with The Lakes and start to settle, and save them another upheaval. But she'd been more than a little twitchy.

Jasper pawed at his leg and made puppy eyes at him. Fraser sighed and grabbed the lead and poop bags and pulled on his coat. 'Okay, let's go get Lily. We can take her on a walk too. Maybe with you in tow she might actually smile.'

They trudged up the road to Joe and Rose's house. Rose tugged the door open. 'Hey, Fraser. Hey Jasper!' She bent and nuzzled the dog's fur. 'How's things?'

'Not bad.' *If only she knew.* 'We've come for Lily.'

'Lily?' Rose straightened and frowned. 'She's not here.'

'Oh. Maybe she's back at home and we somehow missed her. What time did she leave?'

The frown turned to concern. She put her hand on his arm. 'Fraser, Lily hasn't been here since last week.'

'What?' His heart stumbled. Something was wrong with this scenario. Very wrong. 'But she told me last night she was babysitting Katy. Staying over like last weekend for the hen and stag parties.'

'No. Sorry.' Rose pulled her brightly coloured crocheted wrap tightly across her body and shivered, her expression reflecting the worry whirling in his chest. 'Where is she?'

'That's exactly what I want to know.' It was too early to panic. Wasn't it?

He ran back to the house and up to her bedroom, checking for clues. Bed not slept in. He pulled open the wardrobe door, scanned around.

New backpack gone. Some of her clothes too. No note. No clues to follow.

He sent her a text message.

Lily. Where are you?

And then another.

Please let me know you're safe. I'm not angry. I just want to know you're okay.

Nothing.

He called but her phone just rang out.

Should he phone the police? And say what? *My tearaway daughter has torn away again?*

She'd packed bags, it had been intentional… The police would just tell him to wait. He decided to give it an hour or so and see if she responded to his calls.

He drove around the village and then out into the snow-covered hills, wondering if she'd decided to go for a walk. But without Jasper? That wasn't Lily.

He texted her again. Called her once. Twice. Twenty times.

Nothing.

Nothing for three and a half hours while he lost the plot. He paced. He ran. He searched her room again for any hints as to where she'd gone, knowing the truth in his gut but not wanting to believe she'd actually done it. The too-familiar emotions of helplessness and anger rolled through him. This was his fault. He should never have brought her here when her life was so far away.

He'd pushed her to this.

At twelve forty-five his phone rang. A landline number. London.

'Hello?' He knew he sounded gruff, tried not to, but desperation made him panic. 'Lily? Lily, is that you?'

'It's Police Officer Singh from the Metropolitan police. I have a Lily Moore here to speak to you. Hold the line.'

'Okay. Thanks. But what—?' The police. What the hell had happened? He closed his eyes and remembered all the promises he'd made to Ellen to keep their baby safe. His imagination ran riot with myriad scenarios and none of them were good. He held his breath… There was a muffled sound then, 'Daddy?'

'Lily?' His heart went into meltdown. She sounded scared and so far away. 'Oh, my God. Are you okay?'

'Not really.' Her voice was meek and wobbly. 'Can you come and get me?'

The anger melted away and he knew he'd go to the ends of the earth for his daughter. Although he'd gone way beyond the end of his tether. She'd lied. She'd sneaked out of their home. Other parents would think about leaving her to face the consequences. 'Where are you?'

'Clapham.'

As he'd thought. 'I'm coming right now.'

'I'm…' he heard the sob and it just about broke him '…at the police station.'

'I know. I know, Lily-Bee.' He closed his eyes. 'I'm on my way. Don't say or do anything until I get there, okay?'

'No. Please. Come soon.'

'I'm on my way, baby.' His voice caught. He almost slid on the icy path as he ran outside, coat hanging off one arm. He jumped into the car and sped down the road. At the T-junction at the end of the village he pulled up short and more dread slithered into his gut as he remembered the scan. Two o'clock. He'd never get to London and back and make it in time. He had a choice to make. A choice that whatever he did would hurt someone he didn't want to hurt.

Turn right for Penrith to go to watch the scan of his new baby. Turn left to London to save his daughter.

He wasn't coming.

That was the truth of it. When it had gone way past her appointment time and he hadn't materialised Briana had managed to swap slots with the next patient, but she couldn't delay it any more.

The sonographer was tapping her watch and was clearly not going to let Briana's *traffic* excuse make her clinic run late.

Panic threaded through her as she turned her phone off and settled onto the examination couch. What if something bad had happened to him? What if he'd decided he didn't want to be involved and just wasn't man enough to tell her?

She didn't know whether she should be worried or angry. But all she knew was that she felt something. She felt something for Fraser Moore. Which was even more distressing.

He wouldn't say yes and then not turn up without a reason. There had to be a reason. Surely?

Then all thoughts about him dissolved when the sonographer said, 'I can see the heartbeat. Look, right here.'

Briana turned to look at the screen and saw the little glowing blob. Her heart almost drowned in a surge of love. 'Oh. Wow. It's real.'

'There's not a lot to see at this stage, but do you want a picture?'

She wanted a damn baby-of-the-year award because this tiny little dot was so beautiful and so clever to have got this far already. She wiped her eyes, felt the dampness on her cheeks. She hadn't realised she was crying. But, *oh*. Who knew you could feel like this for someone you'd never even met? 'Yes…' she managed. 'Yes, please.'

'One for Dad too?'

Briana thought about the panicked look in Fraser's eyes when the pregnancy truth had dawned on him and realised that, no matter how much she told herself it didn't matter that he wasn't happy, it did matter. She wanted Fraser to want this baby. 'Yes, one for Dad. Is everything okay? Can I tell him it's all okay?'

'Everything is perfect.'

The scan was followed by her first maternity appointment with a lovely midwife who briefly walked her through the next nine months and handed her more leaflets than she could fit into her handbag. Bloods were taken. An appointment for another scan in a few weeks. Information about antenatal classes. A book about pregnancy.

In every picture the women were smiling.

Now the glow of seeing their baby was dimming a little and the reality of their situation was dawning, Bri didn't feel much like smiling. Fraser had stood her up. Stood their baby up.

And, boy, was she going to let him have it when she saw him next. To hell with being polite and keeping the peace. Maybe next time she'd bring Beth to the scan instead…at least girlfriends didn't let you down.

By the time she stepped out into fresh air she'd been at the hospital for two hours. Exhausted and emotional, she made her way to a café, ordered a cup of tea and some cake and pulled out her phone.

She had two missed calls. A voice message: 'It's Fraser.' He sounded out of breath and there were loud background traffic sounds, the screech and whine of lorry brakes. 'I'm sorry I missed the scan, Bri. I really am. But Lily…she ran away. I'm on my way to London to bring her home.'

She imagined his heart would have been breaking and her own heart clutched at the thought of the hurt and panic he would have been going through when he'd left that message.

Bri inhaled as she listened to his message again.

He'd put Lily before his new baby, and she didn't blame him, not at all. How could she blame him when he'd had to choose a runaway over a scan? It would have been an unforgiving choice for him. But she still wanted to shout at him. She'd needed him there. Wanted him there. And he could have called her sooner and let her know he was okay and to go ahead and not wait.

She sent him a text message.

I got your message. I hope Lily's okay. I hope you're okay too.

She didn't mention the scan because she was so confused about the way she was feeling. But she got no reply. Not for a long time. Not for eight hours. Eight hours of checking her phone over and over. Wondering where he was and what he was doing and why he hadn't been in touch again. Thinking worst-case scenarios. She was starting to imagine what it must have been like for Fraser when he'd discovered Lily was missing. Terrifying. Of course he'd run to her. Just as he would run to any other child of his who needed him.

That was part of his appeal. He was a devoted father.

Then, just as she was settling down to sleep, with her hand nestled over her non-existent baby bump, her phone beeped.

We're home. I'm sorry. Can we talk?

She wasn't sure she could have a sensible conversation at this time of night with all her emotions rattling round her. She sent a message back.

You need to spend some time with Lily.

A pause. Then a reply.

I've just spent six hours with her, most of them in the car where we couldn't hide from each other. Trust me, I'm all talked out with her for a while. I want to hear about the scan. How did it go? Is everything okay? Are you okay? Are we okay?

Her heart tripped a little. She replied.

Embryo is high in the uterus. Heartbeat is good and strong. All looks fine.

She sent him the digital picture on her phone... and almost immediately he replied.

Bri, wow. It's real. Beautiful. A new life. He's got your eyes.

She couldn't help but laugh at that. There were no discernible features at this early stage, just a blob that looked a little like a beating black hole where she would pour every ounce of her love... was already doing so. She sent another message.

Let's hope she's got my brains. And my time-keeping skills.

He replied.

Hey, I've got good brains. I'll work on the time-keeping. I promise.

Before she could think of anything witty to reply her phone beeped again.

I know you're angry and I'm sorry. We need to talk.
Or I need to talk even if you don't want to. Please.

She knew she was starting to soften towards
him again, despite everything. He'd had a day
from hell but still wanted to talk to her about
their baby. He was concerned and contrite and he
thought their little blob was beautiful, the same
way she did, and suddenly he was the only person she wanted to talk to about this.

Before she could stop herself, she sent another
message.

Tomorrow morning? I'm not at work until lunch-
time.

Immediately he sent one back.

Ten work for you? Come up here. I'll make us
some brunch. Thanks again for the picture. x

A kiss.

Which made her think about his mouth and the
way he tasted. The strength in his arms as he'd
held her. The way she felt undone and cracked
open when he was around. The way she felt as
if she could say anything and he'd hold it, hear
her. But, yes, his timekeeping skills needed work.

She sent him her affirmative reply and threw

her phone onto the nightstand, resolutely determined not to think about him any more.

Which lasted a whole ten seconds…

When he opened the door and saw Briana standing there—even though he was expecting her—Fraser's heart tightened. His skin did too. Something fluttered in his chest that felt a lot like relief. Not just that she was giving him a chance to make amends, but more. His life was a mess and about to get a whole lot messier, but having Briana here made it all seem more bearable.

She smiled up at him and his first, most natural instinct was to reach for a hug but he reminded himself that that was not possible. They were walking a tenuous line here and he had to respect that.

'Where is she?' she whispered, as she hung her coat up in the hallway and walked through to the kitchen, and he was immediately grateful she was concerned about Lily and not scolding him about missing the scan.

He followed the sweet, subtle scent of flowers that was so familiar and intimate. 'Lily is in her bedroom. She's grounded and sulking. I would have met you somewhere else for coffee, but I felt I needed to stay here to make sure she was okay. You're going to have to put up with my paltry cooking skills.'

Her eyes darted over to the pans simmering on the stovetop. 'You didn't have to cook.'

'I did. I have a lot of making up to do.'

'You must have been out of your mind with worry.' Her eyes softened and she looked genuinely concerned for him. 'Tell me what happened.'

He poured tea into mugs, plated up the scrambled eggs and toast and brought them over to the table. 'She said she was babysitting Katy. Staying over at Joe's like she did last weekend. I texted her in the evening and said goodnight, like I always do. She sent me a reply with two kisses.' His heart tightened. 'You know what? I was so pleased, so grateful for those two little exes. I thought I was making a breakthrough. Instead...'

He hauled in a breath, reliving one of his worst nightmares. He still didn't know how he got to London without crashing his car. 'She was on a bloody train. Or already at the night club. Or... God knows where. With God knows who.'

'She took a risk saying she was at Joe's, hoping you wouldn't check.' Bri started on the food.

'I guess she assumed that if or when I found out she'd have been long gone. Besides, I don't usually check on something like that. It's her babysitting job and I want her to be responsible for it, but it turns out my daughter's all about the risks. She didn't give two thoughts about lying and blithely met up with her friends. Went to a night club where a fight broke out and she was somehow embroiled. I'm not sure of the details but she was collected up with the rest of them and hauled to the police station. She swears she didn't do anything wrong.' He laughed bitterly. 'Apart from lying to me, underage drinking, you know…'

Bri looked at him and gave him a sympathetic smile. 'She's safe now, Fraser, and that's all that matters in the end.'

'I should have known this was going to happen when she kept complaining about not being allowed to go to London. But I was distracted.'

By you. By our news. And now he was going to have to divide his attention between two children when he couldn't even keep one safe. Here? Or in London?

'I should have read between the lines. She could have been hurt, Bri.'

'I know.' She reached across the table and patted his hand reassuringly. 'But she wasn't.'

'She says she feels trapped here.'

He saw Briana bristle at that, and he knew it stemmed from that guy and that thing in her past she wouldn't talk about. But she nodded and smiled again. 'Maybe I could talk to her? It's about time I stumped up and did the godmother thing properly.'

'I don't know if she'd be ready to listen.'

'I'll listen to her. She needs to feel heard.'

'Sure. Anything. If you think that might help. You know, this is not how I want things to be. Not how Ellen and I planned. Towards…the end…' he swallowed '…we talked about how I should raise Lily. What kind of parent I should be and we both agreed we wanted a light-handed approach. A confidant, a friend, someone who'd listen and take her opinions and feelings into account. And I've tried so hard to be all that. But when it involves breaking the law, I have to draw a line.' He scuffed his hand through his hair. 'By not being that friend or confidant, I feel like I'm not just letting Lily down, but Ellen too. God, I even brought her up here when we'd agreed the city would be a good place to grow up, full of opportunities.'

'Don't beat yourself up about that, Fraser. You weren't to know how things would pan out in London.'

'I would be very grateful if you could try and talk to her. Maybe tomorrow? She'd respond better to you. A woman. A friend.'

She tapped her fingers on the table and thought for a moment. 'I might just have a plan. Leave it with me.'

'And I'll talk to her again later. See if I can break through.' He drank some tea, hoping it would ease the nausea in his gut, and then filled Bri in on the rest of the trip. The police issuing yet another caution and warning Lily it was her last one. The long trip back where he'd struggled to get her to open up. The desolate atmosphere that coated everything.

Bri put her knife and fork down and smiled. 'You have to eat something, Fraser.'

'Later.' He pushed his plate away. 'I'm just not feeling it right now.'

'In that case, can I—?' she stabbed at his toast. 'I'm starving.'

He liked her enthusiasm for food and the fact she was here, helping him hatch plans to keep communication flowing between him and Lily. It was the first time in years he'd felt he'd had someone to lean on. More, a friend who understood what Lily needed. *A friend*. That felt good. He liked her. Not just lusted after her, liked her. That felt even better.

He watched her demolish the toast and smiled. 'That's a good sign.'

'Is it? I remember Ellen throwing up all the time in the first few weeks. I'm not looking forward to that bit.'

'You might get lucky.' His heart tightened at the thought of Ellen's early pregnancy days when she'd lived in the shared student accommodation with Briana, before she'd moved into the flat he'd found for her and his baby. 'We had no idea what the hell we were doing. This time round I'll have more of a clue. Although this trouble with

Lily isn't exactly a good advert for my parenting skills.'

He wasn't sure what he saw flickering across Briana's eyes but she inhaled a shaky breath.

'Bri, are you happy about it?' He hadn't even asked her. God, he was so wrapped up in himself he hadn't been there for her.

She blinked. 'I was in shock at first, I won't lie. It will drastically change my life, obviously. But I'll cope.'

'Which isn't exactly a ringing endorsement. You said you don't want to be trapped. This baby will inevitably…' he dug for the right words '…anchor you in a lot of ways.'

'I don't want to be trapped in a relationship. That's very different from having a child. I want to be able to make my own decisions, be my own woman. I want to call the shots in my own life. And, yes, Fraser, I do want this child. I am thrilled.' Her eyes widened. 'At least now I've got used to the idea.' She laughed and he felt the air between them settle. She was starting to open up.

'Not exactly what we'd planned, eh?'

She gave him a rueful smile. 'The key to life is being flexible. Sometimes you have to admit you've taken the wrong path and reroute.'

'Is that why you came back from Australia? You rerouted?'

For a second she looked like a rabbit caught in headlights but then she nodded. 'Yes.'

He waited. Looked away, trying not to spook her, but silently willing her to elaborate a little on what had happened to her.

She looked down at her hands. 'I thought he loved me, but it turned out he just wanted to own me. I couldn't do anything without his permission.'

'What?' The brief calm he'd felt was replaced by anger. 'Did he hurt you? Hit you?'

'Not badly. But sometimes he was rough.' Her neck flushed red and she rubbed at her wrist where, Fraser imagined, she'd been tugged, pulled or gripped by a coward and a bully. 'He was manipulative. Cut me off from friends and family. Isolated me. Trapped me.' She wrung her hands together. 'I can't believe I let him do that. But he did it slowly and made it sound like it was all for my own good and that he was protecting me and that he loved me so much, that no one would love me the way he did. And I believed him.'

She looked desolate but incredulous, as if she was talking about someone else, not herself. He could barely control his rage. 'He sounds like a monster.'

She nodded slowly and grimaced. 'One day I found myself asking his permission to go to the mall to buy some shoes and I realised my world had become so small and I couldn't get out. He'd trapped me emotionally, physically…'

'I can't imagine anyone doing that. I'm so

sorry, Bri.' Everything slotted into place then. Her determination to be in control of her own destiny, to do her own thing, and the panic when he had held her down.

His gut tightened in shame and guilt along with the anger. And something else too. A fierce need to protect her, to take a stand on her behalf. To make her believe how amazing she was. His heart twisted and he wanted to pull her to him but knew another guy tugging at her would be the last thing she wanted or needed.

'No wonder you want to be in control, Bri. You deserve so much better. If you could see yourself the way I see you, you'd know you are worth a million Tonys. More. You're brilliant. Beautiful. Kind. Clever. Funny.'

Her eyes filled with tears. She blinked them away and laughed, but it was on a choked sob, then she straightened up and looked him in the eye. 'Too right I am. And don't you ever forget it, Fraser Moore.'

His smile came from his heart. 'I have no doubt you'll keep reminding me.'

'Don't worry, I will. Right, I'll clear up.' Stuffing his last piece of toast into her mouth, she pushed her chair back and picked up the plates. More, he imagined, to break the heavy atmosphere than a need to do dishes.

He jumped up and grabbed the mugs, racing over to the sink before she got there. 'Don't. Please. It's my mess.'

'It's my mess too.' She elbowed him away from the sink, her eyes snagging his, and they both knew they weren't talking about the washing-up at all.

He smiled at her, wanting to make everything better. 'We can work it out.'

She sighed and smiled too, her cheeks flushing a delightful pink. 'I'll wash, you dry.'

They got into a rhythm of wash-dry-put-away, working together. Sneaking glances. Smiles. And a momentary sense of peace settled over him. This felt so desperately domestic. Shared. *Good.*

How could the simple act of doing the dishes with someone feel so good? All he knew was that he liked being around her. Even with all this tension. It wasn't just about the baby and having to forge some kind of friendship. The sexual energy between them, fed by memories of that one perfect time, coated everything they said, every look, every smile.

Her movements were so sensual. He watched as she bent to the cupboard to put the detergent away. Acutely aware of the slide of her skirt fabric over her bottom.

He felt himself go hard at the memories of her naked body and thrust his hands into the hot sudsy water to give himself something else to think about.

She straightened and frowned, looking at his hands. 'Hey. That's my job.'

'We're switching.' He leaned across her for a dirty pan as she reached across him for the dish towel, her fingertips skimming across his belly.

With just that slight touch his nerve endings fired into life, his body rippling with sensation.

He looked at her, remembering the way she'd gripped his shoulder when she'd come. The softness of her skin, the taste of her. He felt as if his life was on a constant knife-edge as he'd learned how to navigate his daughter, and now this woman had come into their lives and he was learning her too. Overriding his feelings around her and focusing on the baby was proving to be one of the hardest things he'd ever done.

He turned to face her. So she would hear him. He didn't want to ever see that panicked expression on her face again, or the worry of telling him something that made her feel vulnerable. Didn't want to let her down again. Although he knew he probably would.

But he didn't want to, and that had to count for something. 'I am so sorry I missed the scan, Bri. The minute I got Lily's call I just went into action mode and then I couldn't phone until I stopped at a service station. I feel terrible about leaving you to go on your own. I should have messaged sooner.'

She hugged the dish towel against her belly. 'It's okay.'

'It's not. This is my baby too.'

She smiled and her words echoed his thoughts. 'It's not going to be easy.'

'I'm the king of not easy parenting.' He flexed his biceps and she laughed, squeezing his muscle and raising her eyebrows.

'We'll see about that, Fraser Moore.'

He smiled with relief that she was laughing. 'Are we okay?'

'I am.' She grinned. 'But I'm not sure you'll ever be okay.'

She flicked the dish towel at him and he jerked back. He flicked washing-up suds at her and she screeched, flicking back at him with the towel, chasing him round the table and laughing.

'Hey! Truce?' He put his arms out for a hug, not expecting, but hoping, she'd step right in. She looked at him dubiously. 'Come on, Bri. It's just a hug between friends. Where's the harm?'

'Okay. One hug.' She gave him an eye-roll that would have matched Lily's for condescension then slid into his arms, wrapping her arms around his waist. He held her close. For comfort. For relief. For the pure pleasure of having someone to share this all with. 'I promise I'll be at the next scan. I'll be the best dad I can be.'

'I know you will.'

He rested his chin on her head. 'A baby. Wow.'

'Wow. Yes. A baby.' She edged back and smiled up at him, her eyes misting with heat as she held his gaze for a second. Two. Three. Neither of them spoke. Everything seemed to stop then: his breath; time. All thought. The electricity between them buzzed and zinged and all he saw was a beautiful, sexy woman with an amazing mouth that tasted very fine. And he knew they'd agreed, but it felt as if an invisible thread was tugging them closer and closer. He cupped her face. 'Briana…'

'Fraser…' She tipped her head towards him but a choking, horrified voice from behind made him leap away from her.

'What the hell are you doing?'

CHAPTER TEN

LILY WAS STANDING in the middle of the room, hands on her hips, her face blotchy from crying, mascara streaks on her cheeks. She looked young and vulnerable and utterly shocked. Horrified even.

They'd been making so much noise with their silly game they hadn't heard her come downstairs.

Oh, God, this was not what was meant to happen. None of this.

Briana cleared her throat and tried to stop the hammering in her chest that made her feel lightheaded. Maybe, with the teeniest bit of luck, Lily hadn't overheard their conversation.

'I'm giving your father a hug because he's had a rough few days.' She opened her arms wide. 'I've got plenty to spare. You want one too?'

Lily glowered and ignored Bri's gesture. 'What *baby*? What *scan*?' She looked from Fraser to Briana and back again, her eyes dark and bruised with emotion. Her bottom lip wobbled as the words sank in. 'Oh. My. God. You're pregnant? Dad? Is Briana pregnant?'

Clearly, luck was not on Bri's side today. This year. *This life.*

Next to her, Fraser opened his palms in a conciliatory gesture, his expression flat and giving no emotion away. 'Yes. Briana and I are having a baby.'

'Well, wow.' His daughter inhaled a staggered breath, eyes wide and glittering. 'Don't expect me to congratulate you.'

Bri stepped forward, unsure how to navigate this. Even as a nurse who dealt with kids all day, every day, she felt so out of her depth. 'We didn't want you to find out like this.'

'Tough luck on that front.' Lily shook her head in disappointment.

Fraser gave Bri a small smile of support. 'We wanted it to be confirmed before we said anything.'

'We?' Lily spat the words out. '*We've* only been in this stupid, boring place a few weeks and you're already getting it on with Briana? You're together now, is that it?'

'No.' Briana was definite about that. 'We're not together. It's not like that.' Even to her, it sounded weak and ridiculous.

'I just saw you,' Lily slammed back. 'It looked like you were kissing. You're always going on at me about being honest and yet here you are. Lying.'

'I am not lying.' Now Fraser looked about as torn apart as Briana felt as he added, 'I just haven't been able to tell you yet. Briana only had the scan yesterday. I'm sorry you found out like this, but Bri and the baby are going to be part of our lives from now on.'

'Just great.' Lily threw Bri one last savage look. 'A baby? At your age? And you tell me to be responsible.' She disappeared up the stairs, thumping at every step.

Fraser ran to the door and called out, desperation in his voice, 'Lily! Please.'

They heard the slam of a door, the sag of bed springs. Something hitting the floor.

Fraser's eyes closed and he looked close to broken. There was a long moment of silence. Briana truly did not know what to say except that she knew he was hurting. That Lily was too, and she was desperately sorry for them both.

And also that she wasn't sure she could cope with this kind of drama every day when the baby came along. It was going to be hard enough getting to grips with co-parenting as it was.

Fraser rubbed his hand over his forehead. 'At least we don't have to worry about how we're going to tell her our news.'

'I am so sorry.' Bri sighed. 'That wasn't how I

imagined it going. Do you want to go up to her? Should I?'

'No. Leave her for a few minutes. Let her calm down. Then I'll go up. I think it should be just me for now. But you were right when you said I won't be getting that father of the year award.'

'You just scooped her up from a police station after she broke not just the law but your family rules. She's been your only focus for the last fifteen years. We can't expect her to welcome a baby with open arms, especially when she hasn't got used to the idea of me being around. Emotions are running high. Maybe she'll be better about it when she's thought it through.'

'You think?' His expression told her he wasn't holding out much hope for that.

'Maybe she'll enjoy having a brother or sister around.' She coughed. 'Having said that, my brother never paid me much attention. I was more of an irritant to be ignored than someone to play games with.'

'You have a brother?' His eyebrows rose. 'I didn't know that.'

'He's five years older than me. An accountant, like my dad was. Lives in Reading. We're not close.' Like Fraser, she was short on a supply of people to help her with her parenting journey. No parents alive and a brother far away, although she had her friends here and it was a tight, support-ive community. And there'd be Fraser, of course, doing his co-parenting bit the way he had with Ellen…if he stayed here. And she would be fine and everything, but it just wasn't how Briana had expected her life to pan out.

After Tony, she'd vowed no men, so kids hadn't been part of the picture. Before Tony, she'd assumed she'd get married at some point, have a couple of kids, everyone living under the same roof. But things were different now and with an angry half-sister to her child in tow. None of it was how she'd envisioned her life.

Fraser walked back to the kitchen sink and started scrubbing at a pan. Hard. 'I always wanted a sibling. It was always just me and my mum, but she worked so hard, such long hours—she had a homeware store in Cheshire town centre. I only ever got the exhausted version. No…it was more than that…'

'What do you mean?'

He shot her a wary look. 'I think she blamed me for my father leaving and was always emotionally cold compared to my friends' mums, as if she was just going through the motions. The minute I left home she declared herself free. Like I'd been a brick round her neck. I don't know…' He shrugged, but Bri could see the hurt in his eyes. 'I always wondered what it would be like to have a dad around too, doing guy things, like my friends had.'

'Where was your dad?'

'Don't know. Never met him.' He started to wipe down the sink then moved on to the counter, rubbing over and over at something only he could see. 'She said he'd dumped her when she'd told him she was pregnant. Never heard from him again. I couldn't ever forgive him for that. How could he abandon a pregnant woman? How could he not want to be involved with his child? Coward.'

Hence Fraser's need to be involved with his own offspring. Bri sighed. 'My mum stayed at home and looked after us and the house. My dad was very traditional. Strict. Domineering. All that *Don't speak until you're spoken to* stuff. *Do as I say. Don't answer back.*' She laughed wryly as it dawned on her. 'Then I ended up with not only his duplicate, but a much worse version.'

Fraser stopped scrubbing and looked at her, his eyes were so dark, pain simmered in his gaze. 'I want to hurt that man, Briana.'

'He's not worth your anger.' Her heart squeezed for this guy who was so torn and going through such difficult times but still had space for worrying about things that had happened to her.

Thank goodness she hadn't kissed him. Because that was exactly what she'd been thinking as he'd held her. That she wanted to take him to bed and let him kiss her all over.

This was a big mess. Fraser Moore was one hot guy in every sense of the word and the more time she spent with him the more she fell just a bit deeper under his spell.

What were they going to do? About the baby? About Lily? About these emotions that tumbled between them? And about the raw attraction they both felt and hid from and didn't want to admit? Especially when they were going to have to see so much more of each other.

An unwelcome thought struck her. Would he meet someone else and fall in love? Have a 'proper' family? Would she be edged out?

He hadn't edged Ellen out.

Her heart hurt. It was all so complicated.

She suddenly remembered something Lily had said and couldn't help laughing. 'What did she mean by "at your age"? I'm only thirty-three. It's a good age to have a baby.'

'To a fifteen-year-old anything over twenty is ancient.' He smiled. 'You'll have more clue with a baby than I did at eighteen. And you're a nurse too.'

'I don't know about that. It's a lot easier to teach parenting than to live it.'

'Don't I know it.' He wrung out the cloth and put it on the drying rack.

'Oh, God.' She slumped into a dining chair and put her head in her hands. 'This is a nightmare.'

She felt him kneel by her side, his warm hand palming her shoulders, turning her to him. 'Hey, Briana. It's going to be okay.'

She shook her head. 'I think it's all gone to hell, to be honest.'

She covered her face, said more than a few choice words, then let emotion take over.

He stroked her back but when she made a snorting noise he pulled her hands away from her face. 'Briana Barclay, are you laughing?'

'Kind of laughing-crying, I think. Or crying-laughing. Is that a thing? I'm so confused about everything I can't decide whether to laugh or cry, so I'm doing both at the same time.' She pressed her lips together and tried to stop but couldn't, because the whole situation was actually absurd. 'Lily's right. We were totally and utterly irresponsible. Fine sex educators we are.'

'We were failed by a duff condom. Don't we tell all our students this could happen?' He stroked the backs of his fingers down her cheek. 'It was good, though.'

She felt a giggle burst from her chest and stopped fighting it. 'The sex was amazing, Fraser.'

'Best damned sex of my life. But was it worth all this?'

Worth the heartache and confusion? Worth the nausea that would likely soon start to creep up on her every morning?

She took a chance and took his hand, placed it on her belly. The only bond between them that truly mattered was right there, beneath their fingertips. Worth *this*? She knew without a shadow of a doubt that this baby was worth anything and everything. 'It has to be.'

He stroked his palm over her stomach. 'It will be.'

She truly wanted to believe he meant it. Now, at this moment, when his daughter was safe upstairs. But if he was in London and Bri was here with his other child…?

He stood and helped her up, opening his arms, inviting her in for another hug and… Oh, what the hell, it wasn't as if anything else could go wrong today. It was just a friendly gesture and she needed someone to lean on right now. She slipped her arms around his waist, relishing the feel of his strong body.

She laid her head on his shoulder and wasn't sure whether she was going to laugh some more or cry. Or both. But at least they were on the same side for once. He'd told Lily that Briana and the baby were going to be part of their lives. He'd said it out loud. That was worth something.

Now all they had to do was work out…how.

Warmth crept into Briana's chest as he hugged her close. She'd grown nothing but coldness for him for years, but the thaw was definitely happening.

She just hoped she wasn't going to drown in the meltwater.

* * *

'Still not sure why you want to borrow my puppy, but here you go.' Beth stepped over the threshold of Briana's house and handed Boy's lead to her, clearly confused. 'Care to explain?'

Bri bent and fussed over the dog. 'Good boy. Yes. Yes. We're going for walkies. It's a long story.'

Beth's eyes narrowed. 'I'm an excellent listener and I have all evening.'

Luckily, Briana's phone beeped and she tugged it from her pocket. A text from Fraser, right on time.

She's just left. Walking down towards the village.

She sent him a thumbs-up emoji then turned to Beth. 'Sorry, I have to go. Thanks again for Boy. I'll return him as soon as we're done.'

'Done doing what?' Her friend's voice was imbued with teasing and interest.

Being a godmother. 'Something I should have done a long time ago.' She ushered Beth out, waited until she'd steered her car down the road, then locked the door behind her and set off towards the village on foot. She wasn't sure she was doing the right thing, but she had to talk to her goddaughter.

As for Fraser...well, she'd decided to keep him

at arm's length as much as possible. The hug had been wonderful. And that was the problem. She couldn't allow herself to get all heated up around him when they'd agreed neither of them wanted any kind of relationship. It would muddle everything and make long-term negotiations over the baby more difficult.

It didn't take long for her to see Lily coming down the road, wrapped up against the freezing temperatures, being dragged along by her faithful furry companion and staring at her phone. Briana walked quickly towards her before Lily saw her and made a detour. 'Hello, Lily.'

Lily blinked and looked up. It took her a second to process but Bri saw exactly when it did. The girl's eyes darkened and her mouth flattened. 'This is why I hate this place. You can't get any privacy.'

But Bri was prepared for Lily's reaction. 'I know. I used to think that too. But when my mum got sick everyone rallied round and helped. Left food for me so I didn't have to think about cooking. People are nice here, Lily.'

'Very *friendly*.' The girl glanced at Briana's tummy and shook her head in distaste.

Even though Briana was prepared for it, it didn't stop her cheeks heating. 'I'm not going to tell you it was planned, because it wasn't. It just… happened and now we have to deal with it. You see, adults make some interesting choices too. Not all of them good.'

Lily shrugged. 'Like dragging your daughter to live in Oakdale?'

'Oh, Lily, we don't have some sort of handbook for being a parent. Your dad does what he thinks is best for you.'

Lily harrumphed. 'Did he tell you to say that?'

'Of course not. No one tells me what to do and say, Lily. I am my own person.'

The girl's eyebrows rose and Bri thought there may have been a glimmer of admiration there but then Lily said, 'Are you two getting married now? Or what?'

'No!' Bri willed her beating heart down to a more manageable rhythm. 'We're working the details out. But me and your dad…we're not *together*.'

'You're not even going out with each other? But you're having his baby.'

'No.' Maybe this hadn't been such a good idea after all. 'I mean…yes. It's a bit of a mess, to be honest.' Lily deserved honesty and at almost sixteen she could handle the truth. 'We're having to work things out as we go along. But whatever happens, you will always be so, so important to your dad. Always.'

'Right. Yeah. Sure.' Lily's eyes grew wide and there was a wealth of judgement there that Briana felt keenly. 'Are you here checking up on me so you can report back to him?'

Bri tugged gently on the lead and brought Boy to heel, trying to act as if this hadn't been a planned meeting, even though there'd been a lot of work behind the scenes to make it look like an accidental encounter. 'Not at all. I promised Beth I'd take Boy out because both she and Alex are working late and this little fella needs to work off some energy.'

Lily frowned. 'She usually asks me.'

Shoot. Briana thought quickly. 'We were chatting the other day and I offered, that's all. Which way are you going?'

Her goddaughter shot her a look that Bri interpreted as, *Any way you're not going.*

But Briana ignored it, and laughed at the dogs jumping at each other, barking and chasing as much as their leads allowed. And even though she felt completely out of her comfort zone she was going to follow through on her plan. 'Aw, look. They're so happy to be playing together. Maybe we should take them up to Oakdale Top and let them off their leads to have a run.'

'No, thanks.' Lily turned and pulled Jasper closer. 'Come on, we're going home.'

Drastic times call for drastic measures. Bri took a breath and called to Lily's back, 'I'm not surprised you ran away.'

Lily froze in her tracks then slowly turned

round to glare at Bri. 'Because you think my dad's unreasonable and stupid, too.'

'No.' Feigning uninterest, Bri sauntered towards her. 'I think it's genetic.'

Lily's frown deepened. 'What?'

'Your mum ran away too.'

'When?' A flicker of interest, pretending not be interested at all.

'She was thirteen. She dragged me along too.' Briana started to walk slowly up the hill away from the village, bringing Lily along with her story, as she'd intended. 'That did not go down well in my house, or hers. Not at all.'

'Why did you run away?'

'The fun fair had rolled into Kendal as it did once a year. Our parents said they'd take us, like always, but we didn't want to go with them and come home early like little kids. We thought we were all grown up and wanted to go on our own and stay until it ended. Maybe even work there, do a few weeks on tour with them. I can't even imagine what we were thinking…so naïve. So we planned a pretend sleepover at Ellen's house, then when everyone had gone to bed, we slapped on make-up and sneaked out the window with packed bags, unsure where we were going to spend the night but determined not to come home until we'd had our adventure. We got a taxi into Kendal—which cost a fortune.'

'Tell me about it.' Lily had the good grace to look sheepish.

Briana smiled. 'We got to the fair quite late and it was brilliant. Such fun. We rode the Waltzers and dodgems and ate candy floss. We flirted with the guys who ran the rides. They weren't teenagers like we'd thought but proper grown-up men and we were in awe of them. We told them we were sixteen and they gave us some vodka to drink. Then some more, and suddenly I'd had a lot and I didn't feel great.

'One of the men…' she took a breath, reliving the panic and fear of that night and that stupid decision '…started to put his hands in places I didn't want to be touched. And when I looked around there was no one else there but us four. It was dark and we were alone with these guys we didn't know, and I remembered stories about young girls being kidnapped and I got very scared. And he wanted…well, you can imagine what he wanted, and I started to cry, then I was sick over his shoes. That put him off.'

She glanced at Lily, who was listening intently. 'Thank God for Ellen, who pulled me away and told them where to go. Then suddenly both our mums appeared, shouting at the men and threatening to report them to the police. Turned out the taxi driver knew my mum and had rung her, asking whether it was okay that we were going to the fun fair so late and on our own.'

'You escaped then?' Lily was wide-eyed.

'I've never been so scared in my life, or so grateful to see our mums.' Bri smiled and nodded. 'I was grateful to the taxi driver too, and that I lived in a place where people look out for each other.' Bri stopped talking then, not wanting to sound too preachy.

Lily's eyes sparkled as all this sank in. 'Were you grounded too?'

'Yes. But I was kind of glad, really. I deserved it and didn't want to venture out for a while after that. And it turned out the fun fair wasn't as fun as I'd thought it would be.'

'London is, though.'

Bri glanced at her as they hiked up the hill. 'It can be. But not when you're breaking the rules. Juvenile detention can get old very quickly.'

'I didn't do anything wrong.' Lily swallowed and looked away, the hard act softening and letting a little bit of vulnerability through, even if she didn't want to. They both knew she'd done a lot of things wrong, but it was okay, she was young and had a lot of learning to do. 'Were you scared?'

'When the fists started flying. Yes. I thought I was going to get hit.'

'It would have been so frightening.' Bri thought for a moment, wondering why Lily had put herself in that situation and for who. 'Do you miss your friends?'

Lily's eyes glistened. 'Mmm…'

'A particular friend?'

Her goddaughter bent to nuzzle Jasper's fur and gave the smallest of nods.

Bingo. 'Does this person have a name?'

A long pause. Lily chewed her lip. Looked away and then down at her boots. 'Jerome.'

'Is he…um…?' *What would Ellen do? She'd just ask outright. Surely?* 'Your boyfriend?'

'No.' The denial was too quick. He wasn't Lily's boyfriend, but she wanted him to be.

Oh, poor Lily. In love and lonely up here. 'How about you invite him up here for a weekend?'

That received a look that said, *Kill me now.* 'To Boringsville? He'd hate it.'

'How do you know? He might be a secret fan of mountains and lakes.'

'He likes good music, dancing, that kind of thing. Not hills and trees.' They'd reached the summit and they were both a little out of breath. The dogs chased and ran across the snowy slope.

Lily was finally talking and Bri felt heady with the breakthrough. 'If he likes you, he'd come and stay, right? He'd want to be with you, whether it's about dancing and music or trees and mountains, or anything else *you* might be interested in.'

'I guess.' Lily shrugged.

Briana scanned the vista in front of them. The sun was setting over snow-capped mountains, coating them in smudged oranges and reds. Lights twinkled in the houses in the valley below. Snow glittered on the fences and grass. It was achingly beautiful. But she could see how a teenager might not see the beauty in it. Not yet. Maybe only when they came back to it after years away and breathed it in, tucking the majesty of it all into their heart and chest, let it slip between the muscle and sinew and into the bloodstream and feel it beat through them.

She loved it here and could see why Fraser might have thought it would help his daughter. And it still might. Lily just had to be open to the opportunities here.

Briana looked at an outcrop of limestone on their left. 'Have you explored those caves over there?'

'No.' Lily followed her gaze.

'There are glow-worms in there. It's amazing. Magical. Tiny microcosms of life, glittering in the dark. You'll have to take Jerome to see them.' She laughed. 'I bet you don't get many glow-worms in Clapham.'

'No.' Lily snorted. 'We have some pretty cool vintage shops, though, and a good market.'

'Oh, yes, London's great for shopping, I'll give you that. But we do have great markets in Keswick and Kendal.' Bri thought for a moment. 'I know! My friend Phil runs the outward-bound centre in Bowness. He does canoeing, caving and bush skills. I could ask him for mate's rates if you like, so it doesn't cost too much. Are there many caves in London?' A chill breeze was whipping round them and Briana huddled closer to Lily so they could hear each other's words.

Lily smiled and shuffled an inch towards Bri. 'No, but it sounds cool.'

'And there's mountain biking. Movies if it's raining. The climbing wall. There's heaps to keep him busy. And, of course, there's you. More incentive to come here than anything else, right?' Briana took a chance and, smiling, tucked a stray strand of Lily's hair back behind her ear, the way she had back when Lily had been six years old. 'Ask him up for the weekend.'

'Dad won't let me.' But her eyes were brighter. She was thinking about it.

'Have you asked him?'

'I'm grounded. I can't do anything.'

'Give it a try. Tell him how sorry you are about London—you are sorry, aren't you?'

Lily nodded, her eyes glittering with tears. 'Yes.'

'You know he loves you. Very much. He just wants you to be safe. And happy.' She tried to be tactful. 'Drugs and stealing and fighting won't make you happy, Lily. They'll give you a buzz that's here and gone in a heartbeat and leave you craving more excitement and more buzz, and it won't ever seem enough. And they won't make you happy in your bones.'

Lily's eyes rolled as if she'd heard this a million times already.

Well, tough. Briana was her godmother and it was her duty to say it too. But she took the hint and turned the conversation back to the boy. 'Good relationships make you happy, you know? When you feel as if you're on the same wavelength as someone and you make each other laugh and you can be totally honest.' Bri's heart twinged, wishing she was able to walk her own talk with Fraser. She felt so connected to him and that scared her more than anything. 'And if Jerome likes you, he'll want to make you happy too. Invite him up.'

Lily thought some more and then her mouth curved into a full, open, excited smile. 'Maybe…'

Bri grinned too, feeling as if she'd finally done something good.

It wasn't exactly a yes. But it was a whole lot better than a no.

CHAPTER ELEVEN

FRASER WAS GLAD when half-term came to an end and he wasn't forced to bear the heavy atmosphere of a sulking daughter all day. He was also unbelievably buzzed to see Briana.

Because of the baby, he tried to convince himself.

But he hadn't realised that working alongside someone who was carrying his child wasn't easy. He tried not to panic as she was jostled by kids rushing along the busy school corridor, or to fuss when she was almost hit by an errant basketball when she crossed the outdoor court. He tried not to stare at her belly, still not able to believe this was all real.

Mostly, he reined in his desire to just spend time with her. Because he'd come to realise that spending time with Briana made him want to spend more time with her—and not in a hands-off fraternal way—and he knew if he blurred that line, they'd all get hurt in the long run.

But here they were, back in the school clinic,

and his heart did its customary flip when she smiled at him. He was trying to concentrate on a pastoral care meeting about a troubled truant but all he wanted to do was gaze at the way the winter sun caught strands of copper in her otherwise blonde hair. He'd never noticed that before.

'I'm doing a home visit after our outreach clinic,' Bri said. 'The mum rang saying Marco has been having stomach pains on and off for a few weeks but is refusing to go to the doctor. I'm just going to go and assess the situation. See if the abdomen pain is real or just an excuse to stay off school.'

'I'll come with you.' Fraser jumped in. 'I can expedite any referrals if necessary.'

Her eyebrows knitted. 'I think I can handle this on my own, thanks, Dr Moore.'

He could see he'd irritated her for some reason, but he didn't care. 'In London, we tried not to go on home visits alone to people we hadn't met before. Safety comes first. Always.'

Amira, the school counsellor, nodded in agreement. 'I think that's wise, Bri. You don't know what you're going to come up against these days.'

Briana visibly bristled. 'I'm quite confident I'll be okay. I've done lots of home visits with no problems.'

'Then you can show me the ropes,' Fraser said. 'Introduce me to some of the local clients.'

Bri frowned at him then closed her notebook

and nodded. 'We'll leave here at four-thirty. I'm sorry, I have to run, clinic starts in two minutes.'

Four hours later they were sitting in Bri's car, driving back from the home visit. She hadn't said much since the meeting and he knew it was because he'd insisted he go with her. So he started with an apology. 'Hey, about earlier… I didn't mean you couldn't handle the situation. You were awesome in there.'

'I don't like being undermined in my job and I thought two of us going would be over the top for a stomach ache.' She steered the car carefully along a winding country road and kept her eyes facing forward. 'As it was, I'm glad you came. Marco really opened up to you while you played that video game.'

'My misspent youth finally came in useful. It's a good ploy to get kids talking without staring at them across a desk and making them feel uncomfortable. I'm glad we managed to talk about what's really happening beyond the stomach ache excuse. Poor kid's being bullied and is too scared to tell anyone.'

'Hopefully, he'll attend the meeting with the head of Year Ten and get back on track with his schoolwork. But as he's another of Lewis Parker's bullying victims we really need to address that.' Bri idled the car as they waited for traffic lights to change to green. 'I've already spoken to Mr Wilson about it, but we need to do some more anti-bullying workshops and specifically with young Lewis. Who knows what's going on at home?'

Her shoulders relaxed a little and she smiled tightly. 'How's Lily?'

'I would say, on balance, she's a little brighter.'

Bri breathed out slowly and nodded. 'Good. I thought I may have gone a bit overboard with the lecturing.'

'I can't imagine you lecturing anyone.'

'It's funny, I manage fine with the kids at school but as soon as it's personal I get all tongue-tied and second-guess myself.'

'Welcome to my world.' He laughed, glad that she'd thought Lily was *personal*. 'I don't know what else you said or did, but she's asked if some guy called Jerome can come up and stay at the weekend.'

Bri hit the steering wheel and whooped. 'Please tell me you said yes.'

'On condition she pays for the petrol it took to drive to London and back, doesn't lie to me again, completes her homework on time and does her chores without being asked.'

'You are a hard taskmaster, Fraser Moore.'

'A pushover, more like. But she's been so remorseful about running away, and we made a deal she has to stick to and prove she's trying hard.' He'd been thrilled seeing his daughter's excited face when he'd agreed to the visit. 'God knows what we'll do with him for two days up here in winter—'

'*You* won't do anything except provide a free taxi service and food. Lots of food. And then support Lily when Jerome has gone back to London. She'll either be delighted with how it went or distraught. Either way, you have to be there for her. Not to give advice, just to listen.'

'I'm trying.' It was all very trying, but he had to make it work.

'The truth is, your daughter is lonely and hurting.'

'I know. And it's my fault for bringing her here.' His gut tightened. 'I'm so grateful you're helping me.'

She threw him a scornful frown. 'Fraser, I didn't do this for you, I did it for me and for Lily. I want to spend time with her. I want to get to know her and have a… I don't know, a friendship with her.'

'Hopefully one of us will.'

'You're her father, not her friend. In the end, you have to be the parent and sometimes that's hard.' She smiled at him before looking back at the road ahead. 'You've gone through some very emotional things together. She loves you, Fraser.'

'And I love her so much I don't know what to do with it all. So it comes across as overbearing.'

'I hope…' Briana put a hand on her tummy. 'Oh, nothing.'

'What?'

They pulled up outside her cottage. Bri switched off the engine, inhaled deeply and said on a sigh, 'Forget I said anything, I need to shut up before I start to sound needy or something.'

'You're not. How are you feeling?'

'Rough. Nauseous. Jittery. A bit sore. But it'll pass.'

He'd been too focused on himself and Lily and mooning over Briana's beauty instead of thinking about how she was coping. *Selfish idiot.* 'What do you need, Bri? What can I do to help?'

She waved her hand at him. 'I'll be fine. Honestly. I'm tired and hormonal and starting to believe my own rhetoric.'

His heart hammered. 'Come on, Bri. Please, open up and tell me what's on your mind. We can't do this if we're frightened of what the other person's going to say or how they're going to react. It worked well for Ellen and me because we were totally honest and open. About everything.'

But, he did admit to himself, it had worked because there hadn't been this tsunami of longing hanging over them every time they'd been together. And, he also admitted, he didn't want Briana to be honest and open about any future relationships she may have with other guys, because he couldn't *think* about her with another man.

But Briana nodded. 'Okay. I'm worried that my child—'

'*Our* child.'

She sighed. '*Our* child will be one of those sad little kids who lugs a suitcase across the country to see a parent. Half-term holidays. One weekend in four. It'll be heartbreaking for us both. I haven't had the baby yet, and already I can't bear to think of being separated from it.'

'Then we'll have an arrangement like Ellen and I had. One week with you, one week with me.'

'London and the Lakes? Really? What about schooling?' Briana blinked rapidly, her hand on her chest, over her heart. 'That's not going to work.'

'No. You're right.' If he stayed here he'd break Lily's heart, if he moved back to London things between him and his new baby would be rocky from the start. Never mind things between him and Briana. 'It's difficult, I agree. I've made no firm decisions about moving back to London. We just need to be honest and open and clear about our expectations and intentions.'

She nodded. 'It sounds so transactional. Like a business agreement.'

'It has to be.' It was the only way he was going to survive this. 'Ellen may not have told you, but we drew up a contract just to make everything clear. That way, we both knew what was expected.'

'It's a baby, Fraser. Not some kind of product or a service.'

'Do you have a better solution? Because, trust me, things could get messy further down the track when you meet someone else and you decide to get married or move away.'

She shook her head quickly. 'I won't.'

'How do you know? We can't see into the future. We can't make those sorts of promises. You might meet someone and fall in love and move across the world, not just the country. Or I might. And then what will happen to access and custody? We have to protect ourselves. And our child.' His heart squeezed at the thought of that tiny thing growing inside Briana, and her possessive protection of it, and simultaneously seized at the thought of her having a future that didn't include him. 'We have to have things in writing. I can't promise it's going to be easy, but I do promise I will help in every way I can and that you can always talk to me.'

She nodded. 'You should know I'm not always going to agree with the things you do or say when it comes to raising our child.'

'I have no doubt we'll have a lot to work out and I'll be there every step of the way.' He thought for a moment and realised he was looking forward to sparring with her even if, somehow, he'd have to work out a way of existing and not wanting to touch her or kiss her.

She finally smiled. 'In which case, we need to think of some names. That's the fun part, right?

Hell knows, I could do with some fun right now. Any ideas?'

She casually put her hand over his and he felt the rush of heat that happened every time he touched her. She blinked up at him through thick, dark lashes and he saw the bloom of pink on her cheeks. The last time he'd seen that she'd been coming down from an orgasmic high he'd given her. And, *man*, he really needed to kiss her. That would at least expunge this ache that never seemed to dim no matter what he said or did. And, at the same time, cause a whole lot more problems. But they were already so deep in complications he didn't think a few more would make much of a difference.

No.

He wouldn't initiate anything. But the longer they sat looking at each other the more the tension ratcheted up. Kiss or not kiss? Speak or not speak? Truth or denial?

Just to break the silence he said, 'Josie for a girl. After my mum. Vincent for a boy. Or Pep. I like Pep.'

'Pep? Vincent?' She looked confused. 'Unusual names.'

'Not if you're a football fan.'

Her eyes widened in horror. 'I am not naming my son after a football player.'

'You would if you knew how brilliant they are.

Imagine the kudos of being named after the captain of the best football team in the entire world.'

'Vincent is kind of growing on me.' She smiled, but she didn't move her hand. 'How about Adele for a girl?'

'After the singer?' He shook his head. 'In that case, what about Lady Gaga? Or Madonna?'

'Maybe we could go for something a little less…unique?' She laughed, then she looked at him and her expression softened and she stopped laughing and bit her lip.

His eyes were drawn to her mouth, but he forced his gaze back to her eyes. There was so much emotion in there…he could see the simmering attraction, the confusion, and the struggle. Mostly, he could see the heat he knew was mirrored in his face.

If they had been two normal people about to get things on, it would have been the perfect time to lean in and kiss her, but because their situation was far from normal he swallowed and exhaled.

But it didn't have the required effect of switching off his libido. Or his feelings. Because thinking up baby names conjured up happy families and they weren't going to do that.

Even though he wanted to.

Yes. He wanted to. He wanted her. Despite all the problems that would entail. Despite the fact she didn't want to. Despite that committing to something scared the heck out of him. He wanted

Briana in his life in a more committed way than co-parenting.

Which made him more of an idiot than he'd realised.

He was going crazy.

'Are we having fun yet?' His voice was all gravel and growl.

Her eyes misted. 'Getting closer.'

I wish. That thought rattled him. No matter how much he tried to keep away from her, he just couldn't. 'Briana, what do you want from me?'

'I told you. I want you to care for and about our child.'

'But this?' He looked down at their hands. Somehow they'd gone from her palm covering his hand to intertwined fingers. Her thumb ran gentle circles over his skin. 'What about *this*?'

She quickly slid her hand away and held it against her chest. 'I don't know.'

'Me neither.'

'I should go.' She shook her head, turned to get out of the car again, but he put his hand on her shoulder. 'Don't run away, Bri. It's all still going to be there even if you pretend it isn't. We have to talk about it.'

'Do we?' Her voice was raw with emotion. 'Can't we just hope it all just goes away?'

'You ever get tired of doing that?'

She glanced back at him, her expression telling him to back right off, so there was no reason for him to stroke her arm and coax her back. But he did.

Her expression also told him she was as rattled as he was about the potent connection between them that had him searching her out, aching to see her, wanting to kiss her.

He nodded as she turned back to him. She was staying, at least for now. He took her hand again. 'This is some kind of intense stuff, right?'

'It's ridiculous, to be honest. I can't believe I'm even acting like this.' She breathed out heavily and sat back in her seat. For a moment he thought she was going to change the subject, but she eventually nodded as if she'd come to a decision. 'Thing is, Fraser… I'm so confused. I swore I wouldn't ever fall for someone else and yet here I am, sitting in my car on a freezing winter's night, wanting you like I've never wanted anyone before. I don't need a man in my life. I don't want to feel less than…worthy all over again, not when I've finally clawed some self-respect back.'

He wondered why she'd decided to be so honest with him when she'd been reticent before, and hoped it was because she was starting to trust him. He tilted her chin so he could meet her gaze. 'You are worth so much.'

'I don't want anyone to have a hold over me, but the moment I see you I feel…captured. But not in a bad way, well…not much.' She laughed shyly as her hand fluttered across her face. 'I'm not making sense.'

She didn't want a relationship but she wanted him. His heart thudded a weird rhythm against his chest wall. 'There's a lot of stuff going on here…like this baby, like Ellen and Lily and our past. Your reluctance to trust, me not knowing how to navigate any of this and doing everything badly. But cut through all that and, well… I like you, Bri. I have no idea what the hell is going to happen between us and I'm probably going to regret saying this, because I know you're just going to walk away, but… I want you. That's the easiest part of it.'

'Is it?'

'You want to see?'

'I…' She tilted her head towards him, and he saw the need in her eyes, the tremble in her hands. 'Yes.'

He slipped his fingers into her silk-soft hair, then his mouth covered hers. He felt her initial uncertainty, then heard a guttural mewl of pleasure as she opened her mouth and it almost broke him.

The kiss started out gently, but she pulled him closer, angling her head and slipping her tongue into his mouth on a moan.

As the kiss deepened, he felt the kick in his gut and the tightening of his skin. Desire wound through him along with the sense that he'd both come home and yet was exploring an exotic foreign place. A need to commit every nuance, every taste, every sensation to memory because he didn't know if he'd ever get the chance to return.

Then he didn't think at all, just learned her again, getting lost in her taste and her moans and the caress of her skin against his. He wanted to drown in her. To anchor himself to her. Their gasps became frenzied. She grasped his face, kissing him hard and deep.

But when he tried to pull her over the gearstick she laughed and pulled away. 'Whoa.'

Her whole body was shaking and he ran his hands down her arms to steady her…or steady himself, he wasn't sure which. She bit her bottom lip and rested her forehead against his. 'We probably shouldn't have done that,' she said, breathless and wide-eyed.

'I can't get enough of you, Bri.' It was his truth and he knew it might scare her away, but he couldn't live without saying it, or without her knowing it. What she would do with that knowledge he didn't dare think about.

Her palms were on his chest as if she wanted to push him away but couldn't summon the strength to do it. Her eyes were still slick with desire, but her words were fierce. 'Now, yes. But what about in a year? Or three? I don't want to bring a baby into a minefield that's going to blow up any time.

It's going to be difficult enough with shared parenting in two different houses.'

'So move in with us.'

'What? You're definitely staying here, then?' She looked almost as surprised as he felt after the words had tumbled out. But he couldn't take them back. And, just as suddenly, the image of her all beautiful and pregnant and in his bed loomed into his head. Then a picture of a happy family…but she didn't want that. It was clear from her face. So why he kept on talking, he didn't know. Why they'd kissed, he didn't know…not any more. She'd been right. It just caused a lot more problems.

But, *man*, it had been one stellar kiss.

Was he going to stay here? 'It's a big house. We have space. A room for you, and another one we could turn into a nursery.'

Her expression softened but she kept on shaking her head. 'No. No way. I'm fine in my cottage. I have room for a little one. I'm going to change my study into a nursery.'

He felt himself free-falling from the passionate high to a slump of reality and he should have been glad she didn't want anything material from him, but a heavy weight settled in his chest. 'You seem to have it all planned out.'

'Not totally, but I've been looking online at babies' bedrooms and I'm getting some ideas.'

'Well, the offer is there. If you need help moving furniture or decorating, let me know. I'm a dab hand with a paintbrush.'

Bri rubbed the back of her neck and grimaced. 'I wish Ellen was here. She'd nudge me and tell me to pull my head in and take you up on the offer.'

'I wasn't suggesting you move in…with me. Like a relationship. Just that it would be more convenient.' Sheesh, he was making things worse, pedalling backwards from his off-the-cuff comment.

'Don't panic.' She patted his arm. 'But—and I mean this totally sincerely—I don't think Lily would cope with me being around twenty-four seven. I think she sees me as interfering. I'm expecting her to say something along the lines of, "You're not my mum, you can't tell me what to do."'

'She misses her mum. More than she lets on.'

Bri smiled sadly. 'I miss her too.'

'So do I.'

He knew Ellen would have encouraged him to have a relationship with Briana. *'Life's too short,'* she'd said in her more lucid moments. *'Promise me you'll find someone and make a life. A proper life with a proper partner and lots of babies. Lily shouldn't be an only child like you were. She needs to learn how to share.'*

And, contrary to all he'd agreed, Lily hadn't shared him with anyone ever since. But now…?

He had no choice but to share his life with this new baby, if not with Briana. 'I've been showing her old photographs again and we've been talking a lot about what Ellen was like before she got sick.'

'What does she remember?'

'Snapshots really—her sense of humour, her restless energy before the headaches started. We thought it was migraines, you remember? Then she was diagnosed with depression. She changed so much in a year. Lily tried to understand, she really did. But when you're a child, how can you be expected to understand or make allowances for the strange behaviour of the people who are supposed to protect you?

'Ellen became…unpredictable. Up one day, dancing and singing, and down the next, refusing to get out of bed. That's not good for a kid, they thrive on routine and predictability. As a result, Lily doesn't trust people easily, expecting them to change their minds or be different tomorrow. So I'm glad she listened to you about inviting Jerome up. You're good for her.'

Her eyes brightened. 'I hope so. I wish I'd known how bad it was getting for you.'

'I wish I'd told you.' He wished they could get through an afternoon together without wanting to rip each other's clothes off. He wished they didn't use Lily as an excuse. He wished they weren't both so stupidly scared of taking a risk and seeing where this attraction might take them.

He opened the car door and climbed out into the cold night. 'So many wishes, Bri, and none of them are going to change a single thing.'

CHAPTER TWELVE

GIVEN IT WAS only the end of February, the sun was remarkably warm on Bri's face as she waltzed out of the designer clothes shop on Saturday morning with her new outfit in a smart brown paper bag.

Across the street, early snowdrops dotted the gardens with little pops of white and the sky was a cloudless dazzling blue. It was beautiful and fresh with a definite feeling that spring was just around the corner.

But Briana wasn't thinking about the colours or the flowers. She was thinking about that kiss in the car and the fact they hadn't discussed what that meant for them in the future.

Fraser seemed to be willing to talk about these things, but she still found it hard to be that open. Suggesting to Lily that a relationship was good when you were able to be truly honest with someone had made Bri think—could she ever be that honest? Had she ever felt comfortable enough with a man to truly voice her own needs and wants?

She'd managed it with Fraser when they'd been in bed. She'd told him she'd wanted his kiss. She'd said a few things the other day that made her cringe with embarrassment... *I feel captured. Not in a bad way...*

But it had felt good to put voice to the way she was feeling and not have to pretend otherwise, even if she'd been surprised he hadn't run away right then.

But Bri didn't want to put a name to the emotions in her heart when she looked at him, when he kissed her or made her laugh. So how could she be truly honest with Fraser when she didn't want to be honest with herself?

She sighed and realised she'd stopped outside a nursery supplies shop. A beautiful carved wooden cot and soft patterned fabrics filled the window. A little row of pastel rainbow bunting hung above them and it was so lovely and whimsical it made her sigh.

She ran her hand over her belly and said silently, *That's what I'll do for you. Bunting and rainbows. In our house. Just you and me.*

And there was another thing: when Fraser had suggested she move into his house her mouth had said no but excitement had fizzed through her body at the thought of them all living together.

But the idea, while wildly tempting, was also

ridiculous. She wouldn't be able to emotionlessly co-habit and co-parent like Ellen had done, when all she could think about was how good he made her feel. It would be torture to be around him the whole time. But she was going to have to get used to it. Somehow.

A sudden tap on her shoulder made her freeze. Her breath caught, her thoughts stopped. Panic crept through her veins. Tony? Was he here? Had he found her?

She slowly turned round and breathed out. She was so glad to see Fraser. So unbelievably relieved. 'Oh, Fraser. It's you. Hello.'

He frowned but pressed a kiss on her cheek as if it were the most natural thing in the world. 'You okay? You look very pale.'

'Sorry. Yes, I'm fine. I was miles away. You made me jump.'

He looked at her with concern. 'Do you need to sit down?'

'No. No. I'm fine Honestly.' She blinked and turned away from his piercing gaze. He knew she was not exactly being straight with him but at least he didn't ask why. 'What are you doing here?'

Stupid question, really. While Oakdale had a little corner shop, a newsagent and a post office, Bowness was their closest shopping centre.

'Stocking up on man food for Jerome.' He held up a bulging hessian shopping bag. 'That boy can pack away a decent amount. I've just dropped them off at the outdoors centre for a bush craft day. Starting with canoeing down the lake, then building their own shelter and cooking lunch on an open fire, then playing with knives or something this afternoon.' He winced. 'They tell me it's quite safe and even fun.'

'Good weather for it.' She laughed. 'What's Jerome like?'

'He's actually okay. Polite and well mannered. Very interested in Lily—not just in a guy way. He talks about how clever she is and her amazing grades at school last year. What a great actress in the school play, how funny. He's smitten. So is she.' He tapped his chest and pulled a sad face. 'And my heart is broken.'

Bria laughed. 'The joys of parenting, right? You'd better get over it or get used to it. You're going to have to be there for her tomorrow after they've said goodbye. She'll be in bits.'

'I know. I bought extra tissues and will make her favourite dinner.' He held up his shopping bag again. 'What are you doing here?'

'Looking for something to wear at Joe and Rose's wedding. I'm so honoured they invited me when I hardly know them.'

'It's Oakdale. You're part of the family.'

'I'm just not sure what kind of a wedding it'll be.'

His eyes narrowed and he scratched his chin.

'Hmm. One with vows… I think. They might mention something about till death us do part. And I'm sure there'll be speeches and possibly dancing.'

'Ha-ha.' She laughed. 'I mean, are we getting dressed up? Or will it be more casual? I'm not sure I've bought the right thing. They're your friends…can you tell me what you think?' She pulled the dress from the bag and showed him the fabric, a beautiful blue silk that reminded her of the lake on a calm, bright summer's day.

He shook his head. 'I don't know. I'd get a better idea if I saw it on.'

'Oh, well.' She stuffed it back into its bag. 'Then you'll have to wait until the wedding day.'

'Or you could try it on and show me.' He smiled, eyes glittering and teasing.

Was he flirting? The thought of parading around in her new dress, waiting for his opinion, made her heart thump. But she was probably reading far too much into it.

God. She was baffled by the push and pull of all this. Didn't know where she stood or what they were doing.

But he looked quite genuine. 'Come on, Bri. I've spent fifteen years giving my opinion on girls' outfits. I know not to say it makes your bum looks big and to take my cues from your excited or depressed expression. Although don't expect me to be too enthusiastic unless it's got a skirt down to the floor and a neckline around your throat. At least, that's what Lily would say.'

She relaxed a little. 'Well, you're going to be disappointed, then.'

'I doubt that very much.' Another rakish smile.

That was definitely flirting. His gaze caught hers and she didn't know where to look or what to say. Luckily, he filled the silence. 'What else have you got planned for the day?'

'Not a lot.'

'Me neither. I've got an empty nest, come play hooky with me. You can show me the dress. I'll fix us some lunch, I have more than enough food here.'

This was dangerous territory given their kiss the other day.

But here she was, asking for an opinion and being offered not only that but free food too. If she was going to have to get used to being around him on a personal as well as professional level, once the baby arrived, she may as well start now. Maybe, by the time the little one made an appearance, she'd be completely unaffected by him, just like Ellen had been.

She nodded. 'Okay. Just for an opinion on the dress.' She'd thrown up her breakfast and was now feeling quite hungry. 'And lunch.'

'Great, come up in about thirty minutes.' He grinned. 'We'll have to take Jasper out for a walk too, though.'

'Okay…' It was starting to sound wonderfully perfect. 'A walk and an opinion. And lunch.'

That was all. Nothing more. Nothing to see here.

Nothing to get excited about.

As if.

Fraser opened the door to a smiling, slightly breathless Briana. She was still wearing the bobble hat and jacket she'd had on earlier, but there was gloss on her lips that seemed to accentuate their plumpness and made him think about kissing her. He wondered how quickly they could get the pleasantries over and get her into his bed, given that was all he'd been thinking about since he'd seen her in town. Since before then, to be honest.

Given, too, that their kiss the other day hadn't led to a conversation about a relationship but had left the door wide open for exploration.

Jasper was weaving between his legs while simultaneously giving Briana soft pooch eyes and she laughed. 'Someone's keen for walkies. You want to go now? Have lunch later?'

Someone else was keen to stay in. But he knew he wouldn't get any peace unless Jasper was exercised. 'All right, Jasper. You win.' *This time.*

Briana started ahead of him down the path and waited at the gate. 'Since you're the new kid on the block, I'll show you one of my favourite walks.'

'Be my guest.' He shrugged on his thick coat, clipped Jasper's lead on and followed her cute backside through the village and up the steep incline behind Joe and Rose's house.

But, rather than the serene privacy Fraser had hoped for, the far side of the hill was filled with screeching people tobogganing, snowball fighting and building snowmen.

'It looks like the whole village is here.' He waved at Joe and Rose, who were clambering on a large wooden sledge, with Katy sandwiched between them.

'I'd forgotten this was the best sledging hill in the area.' Bri's cheeks were a delightful shade of blush. 'Tongues are going to wag about us walking here together.'

He laughed. 'Wait until they hear about the baby.'

She cradled her belly over her thick jacket. 'Do you think anyone's noticed?'

'You're not showing yet.'

'I kind of wish I were. I can't wait to get a bump.'

'You'll have some explaining to do. Correction...*we* will have some explaining to do.' He'd navigated it once, he could do it again. People would talk initially, then they'd get on with their lives. There were lots of unconventional families these days. The main thing was that the children were happy.

He thought about Lily and Jerome and hoped his daughter was having a good day.

'I don't care what people think.' Briana cradled her non-existent bump. 'I'm proud I'm going to be a mum.'

You are beautiful. The thought shimmered inside him, but he knew if he said it he'd frighten her off. 'You're going to be a fantastic mum, Briana.'

'Thank you.' She smiled, and he could see she was struggling to keep it from stretching into a grin. 'I hope so.'

He expected her to make some sort of quip about him not being father of the year or her expectations for how he'd be with their baby, but she didn't say anything. She just looked up at him, her eyes soft and misted, her hands on her belly.

His gaze connected with hers and the memories of their kiss, of her naked, of her stunning body tumbled into his head. And, *God*, he wanted to pull her into his arms right there, but there were so many people around it would engender questions from the whole village—and this was where things were so different from his situation with Ellen. He didn't know the answers to those questions so he swallowed the need, turned and trudged on through the snow.

Beyond the gentle slope was a cluster of trees

and a group of teens having a snowball fight. As they neared it became obvious it had turned from a snowball fight to a fist one. The largest boy was bending over a kid on the ground and looking as if he was about to hit him.

Bri squinted and her eyes widened in horror, her hand gripping Fraser's sleeve. 'That's Lewis Parker. The boy who's been bullying Marco and a couple of others at school.'

'Right. This needs to stop.' Fraser marched towards the big kid, who was now rubbing snow into the other kid's face. 'Hey! Stop that, Lewis. Stop it.'

Bri was behind him and hissed, 'No, Fraser. Lewis is the boy on the ground.'

Being bullied himself. *Right. Interesting.* Fraser stopped and took in the scene. Lewis was curled in a ball with blood dripping from his nose. The burly guy was pumped and primed to lash out again.

'We've got to help him.' Bri ran forward but Fraser put his arm out to stop her. 'Do not get involved. Let me handle this.'

Her eyes blazed with indignation, her nostrils flaring. 'Fraser, I can—'

'No.' His body pulsed with adrenalin as he thrust Jasper's lead into her hand. 'Stay here.'

'Fraser!'

'No!' He didn't stop to look at her reaction, but he knew, just by her tone, she'd be foaming with anger. She probably thought he didn't think she could deal with this. He didn't care. He would not allow her to put herself or their child at risk.

He waded into the path of the bigger boy's fist and caught it as it propelled forward. 'I said stop.'

Jasper snarled and barked, tugging on his lead.

The older boy's lip curled. 'You can't tell me what to do.'

'Don't push me.' Fraser glared at him and lowered the kid's fist. 'Whatever is going on here won't be solved by a fight.'

The big kid looked at him as if to say, *No, but it would feel good.*

'I know the local police pretty well. If Lewis wants to press charges, he has two witnesses here, plus your rabble over there.' Fraser pointed to the two other kids who were standing a distance away. 'What's going on?'

The older boy looked at Lewis on the ground. 'He's annoying.'

'So? Walk away? That's what the better man does, right? You're older and bigger. Turn your back. Walk away.' Fraser opened his palms to the older teen. 'But, no, you hit him instead. Not good enough. Help him up.'

Burly boy snarled. 'What?'

'I said help him up.'

There was another staring standoff for one… two seconds and then the big kid put out his hand to help Lewis up. When he was upright Fraser addressed them both. 'Right. Explain.'

Silence.

So much testosterone and very little else.

Fraser turned to Lewis. 'If you want this sorted out you have to tell me.'

Lewis shook his head.

'I'm not going anywhere until one of you talks. You're both wet and it's freezing and pretty soon you'll have hypothermia, which is not fun.' Fraser patted his coat. 'I've got a warm jacket and all afternoon. As long as it takes.'

He caught Briana's eye. She was watching, bent over and calming Jasper. And, probably, taking emotional steps away from him because of the way he'd spoken to her. His stomach tightened. This was not how he'd anticipated their day turning out.

Lewis looked at the snow-covered ground. 'He wanted my money.'

Fraser looked at burly boy. 'Does he owe you money?'

A muffled *'No.'*

'Are you borrowing it or stealing it?'

Silence.

'Right.' Fraser nodded. 'I think I understand what's going on here. Did you take his money?'

'No.' Burly boy looked at his feet.

'Only because you didn't have time. You can apologise for hitting him.'

'What?' Burly boy's eyes grew huge.

'Apologise. Now.'

After a pause where no one spoke, Burly muttered something that sounded a bit like *Sorry*.

'It's not fun when someone older and bigger tells you what to do, right? Even worse when they're talking with their fists, which is the coward's way out.' Fraser turned to the other boys standing with their hands shoved deep into their pockets. 'You two are just as bad for not intervening. Is this fun to you?'

'No.' They both looked at the ground too.

'Lewis, are you okay?' Fraser assessed the kid's nose. 'It's not broken but it's going to be sore. How are you feeling?'

'I just want to go home.'

'That's fine.' He pointed at the big kid. 'If I ever see you treating another human being like that again there will be severe consequences, do you understand?'

Burly boy's eyes didn't leave his feet. 'Yes.'

'Oh, and I work at the school, so expect a meeting on Monday.' He watched them slink away then turned back to Lewis. 'You sure you're okay?'

The boy rubbed his bloody nose and nodded. 'Yes.'

'Who was that?'

'Christian Holmes,' Briana said. 'Year twelve.' He turned at the sound of her voice. Fraser was inordinately relieved she hadn't waded into this. She could have been injured. The baby could have been… He didn't want to even think about that. He cared for her, he realised. So much. Too much. Enough that he was going to get hurt along the way.

And, he thought blithely, it would be worth it. Because she was worth it.

So that made him a prize idiot.

He focused back on Lewis, 'How long has this been going on?'

A shrug.

Long enough that Lewis had been affected and was taking out his frustration and anger on younger kids. A spiral of hurt.

'I don't know what it's like to be a bully or bullied but I do know what it's like to feel helpless, Lewis,' Fraser said. 'I also know how to deal with bullies. In fact, we're running an anti-bullying workshop on Monday for the senior year groups. Hopefully it'll teach you some strategies for dealing with aggressive behaviour. In the meantime, keep away from him.'

'He's just going to stalk my phone and my social media and get all of his friends to do the same.'

There were so many ways to hurt someone these days. It wasn't just playground talk, fists behind the bike sheds. There was cyber-bullying too, which must seem endless when you couldn't get away from it. Then there was what Briana had gone through. Living a long way from home, isolated, threatened and scared.

'Block him, block them all, Lewis. Do not give him the satisfaction of showing him that you're rattled. If you do, you give him all the power. Take it back for yourself.' He met the kid's gaze and saw a wealth of fear and anger and panic, but some relief too. 'It sucks, eh?'

'Yes.'

'So, I wonder if you can help me with the anti-bullying workshops?' At the boy's terrified expression Fraser clarified, 'I just need someone to help me put out the resources, the audio-visual stuff, that kind of thing. Nothing major.'

A shrug. 'I guess.'

'Brilliant. I'll send a note to your teacher to let them know you're helping me out.' Then he chose his words carefully. 'I know you want to make sure this doesn't happen to anyone else, Lewis.'

'No.' His cheeks turned the same colour as the blood on his face. And then Lewis half ran, half walked back up the hill. Fraser only hoped the boy had understood his message and by Monday would have given some serious thought to his own bullying ways.

They were left standing in the lee of the woods, an icy wind whipping round their ears. Fraser wasn't sure how to navigate this now. They'd been getting on so well and then this violent interlude had not only blown that up but had clearly affected Briana.

She was hunched over with her arms wrapped around her body as if protecting herself. His heart contracted at the sight of her. He ran his palms down her arms, unsure at what point it had become his mission to convince her that he was one of the good guys. But he wanted her to know that. To believe him. 'Hey, are you okay?'

She nodded. 'I was worried. I… I thought you were going to get hit.'

'I had it under control.' Fraser smiled at this revelation of concern, his heart still pumping with adrenalin. 'I shouldn't have snapped at you, but I was worried about the danger to you and the baby.'

'No, you shouldn't have.' Her eyes narrowed. 'I do not like being spoken to like that.'

'I know. I'm sorry.'

Her shoulders hitched. 'But at least you stopped the fighting.'

'I've a feeling Lily would have been mortified to see me getting involved.'

'Maybe she hasn't experienced bullying firsthand.' Bri swallowed, her face pale, and started to shiver. 'I really, really hope not.'

'The real work starts with the workshops, right? Giving people the tools to deal with someone like that.' He couldn't imagine how Bri must have felt at the hands of that douchebag ex-boyfriend. A physical and emotional threat that had scarred her.

Something feral uncurled inside him and, without second-guessing himself, he slid an arm around her waist and stepped closer to her. Wanting to protect her from any hurt or harm. Ever. 'I know we're not supposed to be saying this kind of thing, Briana, but I wouldn't have been responsible for my actions if that kid had hurt you.'

'Fraser...' She closed her eyes and leaned her head against his chest, as if she was struggling with something invisible. Then she sighed, and it sounded like frustration more than anything else. 'To be honest, I don't know what we're supposed to be saying or doing at all.'

He got it. There was something important going on between them and it scared the hell out of him. Worse, it felt that whatever it was—especially for her—was so fragile and fledgling that if he pushed her to talk, it would shatter.

He stroked her back, but she pulled away quickly, her hair whipping in the wind as she stood and stared at the spot where the boys had fought. He watched as she retreated into herself, pushing him away physically and emotionally, and wondered what she was thinking. Where she'd gone.

Australia.

He dropped his hand and started to hike back up the hill, putting some fun back into his voice.

'Come on, then. Let's go get some food, you must be starving.'

'I'm not really sure I could eat a thing,' she whispered, but he heard it.

The walk back to his house was quiet, punctuated only by the squeak of their boots on the fresh snow and the panting breath of his Old English sheepdog.

Fraser quickly fixed lunch while Bri sat with a cup of tea, then he served up, all the while the tight ball of tension in his chest seeming to get bigger and tighter. Everything had been going so well and now he felt as if they'd retreated into their own private worlds.

And he ached, more than anything, to be allowed into hers.

CHAPTER THIRTEEN

THEY ATE OUTSIDE in his cosy sheltered garden, a weak wintry sun and a gas heater overhead, with blankets on their laps. The food was good. The view, of Fraser, was amazing. Beyond him were snow-capped mountains, a breathtaking wide blue sky. Space.

It would have been wonderful were it not for this chasm of emotion and confusion between them. She'd been spooked by the fight and the aggression in those boys but, more, she'd been spooked by the way Fraser had looked at her when he'd shouted—as if she was worth saving, as if protecting her was his calling. And she didn't know how to handle that.

She didn't want to be protected, didn't need it. Didn't want any man to think he owned her. But Fraser wasn't like that. He'd been scared for her and the baby, that was all. She really, really needed to stop comparing him with Tony, because Fraser was kind, gentle, honest. A good man with a good heart. And great kisses.

And, wow, he'd looked fearless as he'd strode into the line of that boy's fist and caught it.

Eventually, she put her knife and fork down and smiled, wanting things to get back to how they'd been before they'd stumbled across the fight. 'It still feels super-weird having you here in Oakdale. Funny how things work out, eh? If you hadn't had Lily, what do you think you'd be doing?'

'Oh, I don't know. I can't imagine not having Lily. Travelling more, probably. Dating maybe.' He grinned as she rolled her eyes and laughed. 'What about you?' he asked. 'What were your plans before this little one rudely interrupted them?' His eyes dipped to her belly, hidden under a tartan blanket, and he smiled.

Which made her heart thrill. 'Oh, I was just pootling along.'

'You must have had some kind of plan? Coming back here? What next?'

'Once I came home, I had to heal, take stock of who I was, what the hell I'd been thinking, allowing myself to get into that situation with my ex.' She felt herself closing up at just the thought of him but she pushed herself to talk because that was what friends did: they talked about everything and nothing. 'I was just settling into a routine of work at the school, about to raise my head above the parapet and take a look around. Then…

the rest is history. Now I'm going to retreat behind the parapet again and nurture our baby.'

His eyes slid up to meet hers. 'What had you been thinking? With Tony?'

This wasn't something she generally spoke about, choosing instead to keep it all locked away, hoping she could forget. But seeing that violence today had shaken something loose inside her. She needed to talk about it, finally, to exorcise it from her thoughts, from her bone and muscle memory—to rid her body of the darkness and fear. She did not want their baby to grow with all that spinning inside her. And maybe if she explained, Fraser would understand? Maybe she would too.

Goose-bumps prickled on her skin and it wasn't because of the cold weather. 'At first, I thought I was madly in love. He seemed like a really nice guy. He whisked me off my feet, treated me like a goddess and I enjoyed it. Revelled in his attention, in fact. It was a breath of fresh air after Ellen's death and all the grief and guilt. He suggested we go to his home town in Australia because his UK visa was coming to an end. I thought, *Why not?* What did I have to lose?' It had turned out she'd lost her self-respect, her passion for her job, for living.

'It was lovely at first. Hot. Sunny all the time. He bought me presents, took me sightseeing, refused to let me look for a job because I was supposed to be on an adventure, and he wanted to look after me. I was flattered, to be honest. All that attention…it wasn't something I'd ever been used to. I liked being in his spotlight. This handsome guy who adored me.'

She watched as Fraser's eyebrows rose and thought how ridiculous this must sound. How desperate. But Tony had helped her forget her unbearable guilt for a while. 'I got bored with him going out to work every day and leaving me on my own, so I got a part-time job at the local clinic. He wasn't happy about that. He liked the idea of having me to himself whatever time of day or night he chose.'

'Sounds like a real charmer.' Fraser shook his head.

'That was half the problem, though…he was very charming. At first.' She exhaled as a weight slid into her belly, the dread of those days edging back in. 'He took control of my bank account… which was my fault, I know now, but somehow he convinced me that it was a good idea to have him as a signatory. Then he controlled my spending. Monitored my emails and messages. He became super-picky about where I was, what I wore, who I was with. I didn't meet anyone apart from people at work and he wouldn't even let me socialise with them.

'We started to argue. Things started to spiral. Then…you know what happened.' She rubbed her wrist where Tony had twisted her arm until it had almost snapped. Even though the physical pain was gone, the emotional one lingered, making her keep her distance from everyone.

She looked across the table at this gorgeous man and wanted desperately to drop her guard once and for all. 'The worst thing is I let him do it. I should have walked away sooner or told someone else, but I was so ashamed. I couldn't admit to having let someone do that to me. To control me to that extent. I mean, was I so desperate to be loved that I gave him everything? All of me, my power, my agency and my life…literally?' And she was still giving him time and space in her thoughts. It had to stop. She had to move on before it ruined more of her life.

'How did you get out?' Fraser's hand slid over hers and their fingers intertwined. He was an anchor, a lifeline pulling her from her past and tethering her to the present.

'It ended up being so simple I couldn't believe I hadn't done it earlier. Tony liked to drink. One night I just kept plying him with whisky. He kept drinking. I pretended I was drinking too, but threw mine down the sink any time I had a chance. I was playful and put on an act, coaxing him into bed.' She shuddered at the way she'd used her body. The way he had. 'He fell into a deep sleep and I took my chance, grabbed a few bits of clothes, found my passport hidden in his work bag. And I got the hell out. I prayed that by the time he woke up and found me gone I'd be in Sydney already, or even on my way to England.'

'Did that plan work?'

'Yes. Although I couldn't relax until I was on the plane out of Sydney. I walked the length of that aircraft economy section and checked he wasn't in one of the seats, spying on me. I was alone. Terrified and deliriously proud that I'd escaped, but the fear didn't leave me...not for a long time.'

'You're not concerned he'll come and find you?' His gentle, soft circles of reassurance spiralled through her skin.

'His visa ran out. He doesn't know my address here, only that I'm from the north of England somewhere. The chances of him coming back are very slim. The chances of him finding me are even slimmer. I'm good with that.'

'I'm not. I have a friend in the police force. I'll have a word with him.' Fraser's eyes were dark, his voice cracked and raw. 'If I get a whisper of that man entering the country, I'll be on him in a shot.'

She smiled at the determination in his face. The fact he wanted to fight for her made her chest flood with heat. 'I have no worries about him tracking me or stalking me here. Honestly. I've just got to stop looking over my shoulder.'

He gave her a small smile. 'You were a bit jumpy in town when I tapped your back.'

And she'd been unbelievably relieved when she'd seen Fraser standing there. 'I've a way to go, but I'm getting there.'

'But he still haunts you.'

'If I let him scare me then he's won. I'm so much better, I really am, but sometimes I get caught off guard.' She realised her leg was jittery. She needed to move, to get rid of this negative energy. She slid her hand out from under his, stood up and picked up the plates. 'I'm going to clear up.'

He followed her inside. The atmosphere between them was back to being loaded again, but this time it was different. She felt as if she'd expunged her soul, let him see the very depths of her. She felt naked, exposed. She could feel his gaze on her and she was afraid of what she might see in his eyes when she turned round—thick rage at Tony that she couldn't handle, affection she didn't know what to do with, or pity. So she kept her back to him.

She knew he was closer when the little hairs on the back of her neck prickled.

She felt his hand on her waist, then he turned her round to face him. His fingertips grazed her cheek as his intense gaze pinned her in place. 'Thank you for letting me in. Now I understand why you're so adamant about being independent. Why you're so passionate about stopping bullies.

And why you try to keep everyone just a little at arm's length.' He smiled gently. Softly.

Her heart squeezed. 'I don't know how to do this, Fraser. I know you're a good man. I know you won't do what Tony did. But I'm scared I've built up walls too high to come down.'

'It's okay.' His fingers stroked her back. 'It's okay, Bri.'

Every cell in her body yearned towards him. The arm's-length thing was definitely challenged when it came to Fraser. She put her hands on his chest, felt the steady thump of his heartbeat under her fingers. 'It's not okay. I need to forget it. Put it into the past. Be a different Briana. A better one.'

He frowned. 'Don't change. Please. Don't make yourself into anything other than who you are.'

'But that old Briana let him—'

'No.' He shook his head, stopping her words. 'You trusted him, because you're a good person who wouldn't imagine someone could behave like that. You travelled with him on an adventure because you see the positive in things, and the beauty in places and people and experiences. You had the strength to leave him, even though it was dangerous.

'And the truth is you wanted his attention because we all want that, Briana. We all want to be loved, be liked, to be cherished. There's nothing wrong in that. You deserve to expect that. To be treated properly, kindly and with respect. You deserve so much more. You deserve to be loved and honoured. You deserve the whole damned world, Briana Barclay.'

She closed her eyes, wishing he could be the guy to give it all to her. Wanting that more than anything. Knowing he could be if they both dropped their guard enough to let in the light that shimmered between them.

And knowing that if they couldn't she'd take this moment and hold it tight in her heart. Right now he believed in her. He wanted her. He knew her truth and saw someone strong, not weak. Someone who could trust and care deeply, not someone afraid of emotion and connection. She allowed herself to feel the heat his belief in her generated. To feel her power come back to her, to grasp the adventure again.

When his lips pressed against hers she let him in.

This kiss was different from any he'd ever had before.

He kissed her as if this was the first time, and the last. He kissed her to show her the strength of his belief in her and his promise.

She wove her arms around him and pressed herself against him. He felt her limbs soften, her curves fit perfectly into the hollows of his body. Felt the press of her breasts, the hitch of her breath. Heard the sigh in her throat. And, God, he wanted her so much he didn't know what to do with all the need, all the emotion clogging his chest.

As the kiss deepened he plundered her mouth and she put her hands either side of his face, anchoring him. Steadying.

He didn't want to be steady. He wanted to be rocked, to rock inside her.

He pulled away, breathing hard and fast, took her tight fists in his. 'Briana, I want you so badly I can't even find words to describe it.'

Her eyes were misty as she looked up at him. 'I need you. I need you inside me.'

He revelled in her words. That she could say them to him made him feel unleashed.

'You want to go upstairs?' He kissed a trail along her collar bone.

She smiled, all sex and teasing and hot. 'Yes, please.'

He picked her up and she giggled and screamed at him to put her down. But he carried her up to his room and placed her gently on his bed then stretched out alongside to face her.

'We have all afternoon,' he said as he ran lazy strokes over her arm. But it would never be enough time, he knew, and there would always be interruptions, a reason to stop when he didn't want to ever stop. He ran his palm over her shoulder, but she pulled him down for another kiss. This one was hungry and hot.

He slowly removed her clothes, teasing and tantalising. And she removed his almost reverently. A slow undressing of their inhibitions and fears.

And, *God*, she was so beautiful it made his heart hurt. Soft silk skin, pale from winter's coverings. Swollen breasts and darkened nipples that puckered when he sucked one into his mouth. She writhed against him, her hips so close to his erection he could have slid straight into her.

But he waited. It almost killed him, but he waited. Taking his time to stroke her, to kiss her throat, her breasts and lower.

His heart lurched at the sight of the slight swell of her belly. It was barely a bump, but it was there. A life. He placed his hands there, kissed the softness. *Our* child. His heart swelled at the thought, a tangle of panic and affection for this child. For this woman. 'My darling Briana. You are so beautiful.'

When he looked up he saw tears in her eyes, spilling onto her cheeks, and his gut tightened. 'Are you okay?'

She nodded, pulling him back to face her. 'I am more than okay. I've wanted this for so long.'

He pulled back and smiled. 'What do you mean? Weeks? Days?'

'Oh, come on. You must know I had a crush on you from that first night we ever met?'

'I had no idea.' Geez, things could have been so different. 'Really? On me?'

'Well, it wore off for a while.' She gave him a rueful smile. 'But… I think I'm crushing on you again, Fraser Moore.'

He laughed at her words and the wonder of how life had brought them to this amazing moment. 'Back at you, Briana Barclay.'

Then he kissed her and kissed her and kissed her. Kissed her cheeks, kissed the salty tears away, kissed her nose and her eyelids. Her mouth, her neck. He took his time.

He worked his way down her body, worshipping her with his mouth, his fingers, his tongue. Felt the slick wetness as he parted her legs and slipped his hand between her thighs. As he stroked her there she arched her back, and he watched the curve of her mouth, the slow smile on her lips that turned to the agony of desperation and the pure frenzy of release. Heard the half sob, half cry of his name and felt it deep in his soul, settling there like a promise. Watched it all as if this was a dream. A beautiful dream of touch and taste, of slickness and kissing. Of worship and prayer and vow.

He sure as hell didn't want to wake up.

Then she laughed. A beautiful sound fluttering in the still, pheromone-heavy air. 'Fraser, that was amazing.'

'*You* are amazing.' He kissed his way back to her mouth. 'You make me feel amazing.'

'Win-win.' She laughed. Mouths still together, she climbed on top of him, took hold of his erection and positioned him at her entrance. He could have thrust into her then, but he held back. This was Briana's call. He would follow. Follow her wherever she wanted to go. To the end of for ever.

She moaned his name as she sank over him, tight and hot, her fingernails tearing his skin where she gripped his shoulders. The pain was a thing of beauty, a scar of their lovemaking. A brand.

He was hers. That thought tore through the last shred of reserve he had and wound itself round his heart. He would stay right here for ever if he could. How could he leave her? Their baby?

He would stay.

For a moment she stilled, her gaze tangling with his and God knew what she saw there but she gasped and smiled as tears ran down her face, her palm on his cheek. She sank onto him again and again, taking him deeper until he couldn't hold back any longer.

He thrust hard and fast, gripping her hips, holding her in place. But it wasn't enough. He flipped her onto her back, covering her with his body, sliding into her over and over. Then it wasn't a dream any more, it was real. So damned real it was like a fire burning in his soul, in his bones, on his skin.

His truth was in every look, every touch, every kiss. In the last deep thrust, and in the way he cried out her name.

He wanted more than all day, he wanted tomorrow, next week, next year. He wanted a lifetime. That thought had slid into his brain the moment he'd kissed her belly.

And glued itself to his heart.

CHAPTER FOURTEEN

BRIANA DIDN'T KNOW how long they lay there tangled in the sheets, unwilling to let go of each other, as if this was an end, not a beginning. As if the perfect, glittering spell would be shattered if either of them moved. She fluttered in and out of sleep, half scared of the emotions inside her, half clinging to them.

Her throat was tight and her cheeks still damp from tears. The way Fraser had looked at her, the intense light and comforting weight in her chest, the purity of his kisses…it had all been so much. Too much to feel.

She could love him, she knew. Could give her heart to him…was at serious risk of doing so. They were at a tipping point and she had to choose how this played out. For now she was in control, hanging on by a thread, but it wouldn't take much more of him for her to let go and fall.

Beside her, he lay with his eyes closed, his arm tucked round her body, holding her close against him. His breathing was calmer now and steady. Two things she most definitely wasn't.

She didn't want to wake him, so she lay as still as she could, trying to breathe through a sandpaper throat, and instead of looking inside herself she looked at her surroundings. His bedroom was bright and airy with exposed wooden beams, a luxurious en suite bathroom and a huge window with a view out to the mountains, even from the comfort of his large, luxurious wrought-iron bed.

There was space for a cot, she thought, over by the window. And a rocking chair for night feeding. More than enough space for two people's things. And even for three.

Then she shoved that thought away. She was getting ahead of herself. Thinking things she'd promised she wouldn't think. Impossible dreams. A cot for when it was his turn for the baby. Sure. If he was even still living here and not in London.

God, she wanted him to stay so badly, but couldn't ask him. Couldn't bear to face the rejection.

Her strength was in being on her own, not allowing herself to become embroiled or entangled. Or losing herself again.

She'd fought so hard to survive Tony and to escape intact. She'd spent years with him and he'd won her by stealth, stealing her bit by bit. In contrast, she'd been intimate with Fraser for barely a few weeks...with a large gap in between drinks, and she'd never felt so captured. So captivated by someone's words, kisses, touch. His smile. His laugh.

She'd told him everything and he thought he knew her. But he didn't. He thought she was strong, bold, courageous. He didn't know how scared she could be, how weak. How leaving Tony had taken every ounce of strength she'd had. How hard she'd fought. How few reserves she'd had left, but over the last few months she'd built them up. Impenetrable.

Or so she'd thought.

How at risk she was of losing it all again. How hard she was falling for him, making her vulnerable, making her second-guess her decisions. How broken she'd be if he couldn't feel these same things for her. And he hadn't before, so why would he now?

Her heart hurt at the light and dark. Something warm and beautiful could happen here and she so desperately wanted to reach out and grasp it but was terrified she'd get burned.

She lifted his arm and scooted off the bed. Wrapping herself in his fluffy white bathrobe, she walked over to the window and looked outside.

The light was fading. No beautiful sunset tonight, just a slow slip into darkness.

Her throat felt raw and tight. Her chest was like a vice. She couldn't breathe.

She glanced back at him, his careless slacklimbed pose. His beautiful mouth. That body. Her heart danced. One look at him and everything seemed brighter. But she couldn't rely on Fraser to make everything better. She had to do that for herself.

A bright bubbly tune blared into the silence, making her jump. On the nightstand Fraser's phone lit up.

He lazily rolled over and, not looking, patted around for his phone. His eyes were on Briana. A sexy smile. *Come back to bed* eyes.

And she was, oh, so tempted. It would be so easy to slip back in.

But he glanced at the screen and jerked up, holding the phone to his ear. 'Hey, Lily-Bee, yes, I know. Sorry, *just Lily*. It's a dad thing, okay? You'll always be my Lily-Bee. Good time?'

A pause as he listened.

'Excellent. I can't wait to hear all about it.' His mouth split into a grin. 'I'll set off in five.'

He lay back on the pillow, scuffed his palm over his hair. 'I have to go pick them up.' He patted the space in the bed next to him. 'In five minutes.'

Bri looked at him. 'You'd better get dressed, then.'

'That'll take me about sixty seconds. Which leaves four minutes to play.' He reached out to her and she fought the pull, making herself stay by the window and drink him in.

Seeing she didn't move, he slid from the bed and crossed the room, wrapping her in his arms. His warm body enveloping her, holding her tight against his bare skin. His cheek against hers. 'You don't want to play?'

And, oh, she did. But she smiled, her eyes filling with tears, her throat hurting as she tightened the robe ties around the swell of her belly. She would tell him. Only…not yet. Not when he was heading off for Lily. His daughter needed him level-headed and calm. 'It's okay. I've had a lovely day, but now you have to go and be Dad again. I'll tidy up while you're gone and leave no trace.'

He tilted her chin so he could look at her. 'You never showed me the dress.'

She didn't have the heart or energy to parade in front of him for an opinion or feel his heated gaze on her body. She needed to extinguish the fire, not stoke it. 'Another time.'

'Okay. If you're sure?' He slipped a kiss onto her head, a glimmer of concern in his expression.

Then he was gone.

Much later the next day Briana saw Fraser's car drive past her cottage window en route to his home. From the station, no doubt. Dropping off Jerome.

She wondered how things had gone for the young couple. She hoped it had been wonderful and simple and not complicated and too emotional, the way Bri felt right now.

Whatever happened between herself and Fraser, she had to grow this relationship with Lily. It had been a solemn promise and she intended to make good on it.

She sent her goddaughter a quick text message.

Hey, how was the weekend?

A few minutes later a reply came.

Great, thanks.

She laughed. Teenagers weren't great on detail unless asked direct questions. She hesitated, because it was truly none of her business. But she wanted Lily to know her godmother was there for her whatever happened and however she was feeling.

She bit the bullet.

How was Jerome?

A smiley face covered in little hearts and a big red heart winged their way to Bri's phone. Okay. Now what? She really, really wanted details, but that would be too intrusive. Wow, this was hard to navigate.

She sent a heart back.

I'm so glad it went well.
Thanks for making me invite him. You're the best,
Bri.

And another heart.

You're the best too.

Bri sent two hearts back as a solid warmth settled in her chest.
You're the best.
She hadn't been, but she was determined to be the best she could be now. If she couldn't have closeness with Fraser, she'd at least have a special connection with his daughter. With Ellen's daughter. And that meant everything to her, something to hold onto while her own world was starting to crumble.

She was taking steps away from him.
He saw it in the way she held herself, heard it in her tone and felt it in the way her body had stiffened as he'd held her that last time.
In the fact she hadn't replied to his texts with more than one-word answers for four days. She'd feigned busyness at work and locked herself in her clinic room.

The closer he got, the more she ran. And he didn't blame her one bit after what she'd been through, but he was damned if he was going to let her push him away without a fight.

And, hell, that was one big fat surprise. He'd never wanted a woman like this. Never given so much of himself.

He waited until after the outreach clinic and they were walking to their cars, falling into a conversation he knew she'd be comfortable with. 'The workshops went well, don't you think?'

'Great. Some of the kids are really starting to open up. I think we have a really good anti-bullying strategy in place now. A safe place for kids to come and a shared community direction on where we want to be.' She nodded, using all the right professional jargon that kept him at a safe distance. She looked pale and worn out as she added, 'How was Lily after Jerome went back to London? I messaged her and she said she was fine, but I'm thinking she might be glossing over it.'

He liked it that she had a relationship with Lily, that was something great that had come out of all this. 'She sobbed all evening and we went through two boxes of tissues. I almost rang you for fairy godmother advice, but she cheered up when I promised he could come back again at Easter.'

She rummaged in her handbag and zapped her remote key towards her car, its lights flashing orange in the dark night. Her eyes were skittish and her hands trembling. 'It's serious, then?'

'As serious as it can be at that age. But you know how these things can fizzle out as quickly as they flare.' The way it had between himself and Ellen, but with the additional gift of a baby. He'd put that baby first for the last fifteen years, but now it was time to give priority to his own needs. 'Thing is, I don't want to talk about Lily.'

'Oh?' Briana blinked at him and upped her walking pace.

He matched her step for step. 'Where are you running off to, Briana?'

'Home. It's late. I'm tired.' She turned to open the car door but paused to look right at him. 'I'm sorry, Fraser.'

He felt the kick to his gut like a punch. She wasn't apologising for racing home, or for the awkward, stilted conversations they'd been having.

'What's happening here, Bri?' He put his hand on the car roof so she couldn't climb straight in and drive away. 'We have epic sex…hell, it certainly blew me away. We connected. We did, didn't we? I'm not dreaming it? We have something? And now you refuse to speak to me.'

She shook her head dismissively. 'This is talking.'

'It's polite conversation that skirts around the freaking huge elephant in the room. Briana, I had a fantastic time on Saturday. I thought you did too.'

A pause. A reluctant nod in agreement. 'I did.'

She'd had a fantastic time…he hadn't imagined it. He wasn't in some deluded half-reality where this was one-sided.

'And now?' He didn't think he'd ever felt so disarmed. Raw. Putting himself on the line in a way he'd never done before. 'It seems we're pretty good together and we keep coming back for a repeat performance. So, I don't know about you, but I'm left wondering where we stand. What *this*…' he pointed first at his chest and then at Briana '…is.'

'It's…' She chewed her bottom lip. Her eyes briefly closed, then, 'Fraser, it's not anything. You and me. It's not going to happen. I don't want it. Can't you see? I don't want this.'

And yet he knew if he touched her, if he kissed her, she'd kiss him back. That she *did* want this. And more. 'Don't want it? Or just too damned scared to take it?'

'It's all too fast. I feel things when I'm with you, Fraser. I liked being numb. Cold. Pootling along. I liked being on my own, making my own decisions. Finding out who I am. And now…now I'm unsure. I'm dithering. I'm…' She shook her head. 'I'm losing myself—'

He took hold of her hand. It was cold. Shaking. But her fingers gripped his. Tight. 'You're scared,

Briana. And that's okay. I'm not surprised. You've had a really tough time and this is intense. Hell… you know what? I'm scared too. I haven't dated anyone in years. I've barely thought about anyone other than my daughter for a decade and a half. I haven't chased something for myself. Haven't dared think about any kind of future with anyone.

'Apart from Lily, everyone I've ever cared for has left me. Everyone. I don't know how to do this happy families thing and I tried hard not to care for you. I tried to keep my distance. I tried not to fall, but here we are and in my head I have all these ideas. Images. Hopes.' Yes. He'd dared to hope. 'We have to face it. This thing…it's out of the blue, sure. There's the baby, which complicates everything, but…hell, Briana, we can work it out.'

She shook her head, tears shimmering in her eyes. 'I can't.'

'*We* can.' He put his hand on her cheek. Looked deeply into her beautiful blue eyes. 'I cared for Ellen. She was a wonderful friend and mother and I was devastated when she died. Imagine multiplying that caring by a thousand and learning to hope, but also being torn in half about what to do. Do I hold you close and let myself fall and who knows what might happen? You might die or leave… Or do I hold you at arm's length? That's easy and safe but it sure as hell isn't life-affirming. It's not living. I get you're scared. It's okay.

We can be scared together. We'll be amazing. We'll work it out. Briana…' He hauled in oxygen and smiled. 'I—'

'No. No. No. Don't say it. Please. Don't.' She shook her head, eyes wide and wet. A vehement shake.

Love you.

There it was.

The feeling that had cracked his heart wide open. The tumbling sensation when he looked at her. The devastating need to protect her and the child inside her. His child. Their child. This conversation where his emotions poured out of him and he couldn't stop them.

He'd fallen in love with her.

And she was backtracking so fast he could almost see the vapour trails.

Her face crumpled. She pressed fingers to her lips as if holding her feelings in. Holding her words in.

Words he desperately wanted to hear. That she loved him back. That this could work. That they could make a life, the four of them. Create that picture he had in his head. Where he did the right things at the right time for once. Where he loved her and she loved him back.

That she wanted to try.

But despite whatever her heart felt, her head was telling her to run. She did not want this. Whether she did actually love him or not, she didn't want to. And there wasn't much he could do about that.

He loved her.

He was destined to be by her side for the next eighteen years and more. Co-parenting. Working together. Making decisions, swapping banal grey snippets of their lives. Instead of being a part of them. Instead of building a glorious golden future together. A future he hadn't ever envisioned and hadn't wanted, and now couldn't bear not having. He loved her and she refused to love him back.

His heart felt as if it was being cleaved into two pieces. Whatever happened, one half was hers and always would be. He might as well have cut it out and handed it to her on a plate.

He pulled himself together because she needed him to be okay about this. He wasn't going to push her into something she didn't want. Hell, that's what her ex had done.

But, then, what was he supposed to do now? Smile? Walk away? When his own hopes and dreams were fading and he couldn't grasp at them?

'We're not moving to London.'

'Oh?' Her eyes brightened just for a second.

'I want to be here for our child. I can't miss seeing them grow up. We're staying.'

'And what does Lily think of that?'

'She's not exactly thrilled but she understands.'

'I'm glad you're going to be here. For the

baby… That's good. Thank you.' There was something in the silence she left hanging there. Tears welled in her eyes and he could see her summoning up all of her strength. 'Look, I'm tired. I have to go. I'm so sorry, Fraser. Honestly. I am. I just need to be on my own. It's for the best.'

'Best for who? You? You look devastated. Me? I'm—' *Broken.*

'It's just not going to work.' She let go of his hand and looked meaningfully at him to move so she could climb into the car. There was nothing he could do but step away.

This was it. The end. In a dingy car park on a freezing winter's night.

He wished his chest was filled with the ice that was in the air, frosting the ground, frosting his damned feelings. Filling him up with cold and leaving no room for the bright heat and light he felt when he was with her.

But it wasn't. His chest was filled with Briana. Her smile, her scent. Her laugh. Her touch.

And now…her goodbye.

Briana climbed into the car and took a steadying breath. At least she tried to. Instead, her breath caught in her too-tight chest and stuttered, hic-cupping out on a sob. Then another. And another. She thought her body would implode from the pressure she was exerting just to keep vaguely in control. Reality was she was falling utterly and completely apart.

He was right. She was scared. Terrified. Blindsided by how much she felt for him. How much it hurt to turn away from what he was offering.

She knew he was still looking at her through the foggy window. Hoping she'd change her mind, but she wouldn't. It was for the best, it was. For all of them. This way they could all have a good life, survive. Thrive. Without the constrictions of emotions clouding everything. Without *needing*.

He loved her. At least, that's what she'd thought he'd been going to say. She'd had to stop him, right then, before the words had tumbled out. Panic had exploded inside her. Because she knew she'd have relented if those words had escaped his lips. Knew she'd have walked…run…straight back into his arms.

Knew she would have said it too. Because she did. Despite everything, she'd let him in. And it would be her downfall if she didn't stop it. She'd get carried away with dreams and drop her guard further.

This way was for the best.

It was.

Even though she was going to have to live alongside him for the next eighteen years.

She blinked hard, pressing her eyelids tight closed to stop the stream of tears. She had to be strong. Stronger than she'd ever been. Even though her heart was shattering.

Love.

She would shower their child with it and keep that part she had for Fraser locked away. She would be tortured every single minute she spent with him, and every moment she was away from him. But this was for the best.

She didn't know how long she sat there in her cold car with steamed-up windows, body racked with sadness. How many tears she shed, how many times she asked herself if she was doing the right thing. Whispering to her baby that everything would be just fine. Trying to convince herself.

But when her chest eventually stopped heaving and she could see enough through blurry eyes to drive she turned on the ignition and edged the car out onto the road. Towards her home.

To her future without Fraser.

She might have believed it was for the best, and she only hoped that at some point she'd actually feel it was.

CHAPTER FIFTEEN

WINTER HAD SLIPPED into a warm spring, and today was one of those bright sunshiny days that made your heart smile.

At least, there were plenty of smiles to go around here at the wedding reception, so Fraser imagined no one cared that the upturned curl on his mouth was fake. He was happy for Joe and Rose, of course. They were a special couple and their love and happiness was evident, touching everyone in the room.

Except him. He just felt hollow.

The speeches were finished and the tables cleared away. The happy couple was stepping off the dance floor to a round of applause after their first dance.

Which meant, if he was strategic, he could now slink away and no one would notice.

'Dad, can you at least look like you're enjoying yourself?' Lily nudged him. She looked adorable in a silver summer dress she'd ordered online. Probably trying to make herself look older, but all it did was accentuate her youth. She'd dropped the heavy make-up and was smiling real smiles a lot more. She fitted in well here with all these grinning guests. 'It's supposed to be a happy occasion. Duh?'

'Sorry.' He looked into his empty beer glass. 'I was miles away. I have one of those faces that always looks miserable when I'm thinking.'

He'd been watching Briana across the room, laughing and chatting with Beth. Her hair was piled on top of her head in a messy bun with curls springing loose, framing her face. The blue silk dress was a perfect choice, tight fitting at the bust and flared around her hips. No one would have known she was pregnant.

But he did. He knew her. *Knew her.* Knew she wasn't happy. That she was living with her choice, but it hadn't brought her whatever it was she'd been hoping for. Not that that knowledge made him feel any better. He was living with her choice too.

Lily groaned. 'The resting bitch face excuse doesn't wash with me, Dad. Go ask her to dance.'

'Er…who?' He feigned nonchalance, even though his heart flared at the thought of her.

'You know who. Briana.' His daughter's elbow pressed into his ribs again. 'Go and dance with her.'

'Why?'

'Because she's standing on her own.'

Beth had just joined Alex on the dance floor and was beckoning to Briana to come too. She was shaking her head.

A glance towards him. A look away. A glance back.

He held her gaze as fire ignited inside him. He was angry she'd pushed him away and raging at himself for allowing himself to get into that situation in the first place. He should have resisted. Fought back. But it didn't matter, the love was ever present, a light always there, for her.

He forced himself to look back at Lily. 'I was thinking about going home.'

Lily glowered at him. 'Don't you dare. You're staying here and you're going to have fun.'

He remembered saying those words to Lily a few weeks ago. Oh, boy, had the tables turned.

'What's happened between you two? One minute you're all loved up and next minute you don't want to be in the same room together.' Lily did her exasperated eye-roll. 'This is so not going to work when she's had the baby.'

He rubbed his forehead. 'We decided not to pursue a relationship. That's okay. That's what happens, right?'

'With Mum, yes. But Briana's different. You're different with her. And a lot worse without her.'

'Gee, thanks. But the truth is she doesn't want me around.' He wasn't stupid or a glutton for punishment, and he sure as hell wasn't going to beg.

Lily grinned. 'Could have fooled me.'

'Why?'

'Woman's intuition. Also known as…she keeps looking over.' Lily's eyes settled on Briana. 'She looks sad. Lonely. Even with all those people around her.'

'I know.' His battered heart ached for her.

Lily turned to him, excitement in her eyes. 'So, do something about it. That baby is part of our lives and you're going to see Briana a lot. Are you going to spend the next eighteen years of your life being this grumpy?'

He slumped back in his chair. 'Probably.'

'Ask her out.'

'What?' Was this really his daughter talking?

'Oh, God.' She framed her face with her fingers and shook her head in frustration. 'Please, don't tell me I have to give you dating tips, too.'

'I think I can manage. If I ever decide to date again, which is unlikely.' Root canals had better outcomes.

'Decide now.' Lily groaned. 'You're both unhappy. You both like each other. What's the problem?'

'Why this sudden interest in my non-existent love life?'

'I've been doing a lot of thinking recently. You've spent a long time looking after me and now I'm going to look out for you. Especially as you're slipping into old age.' She winked. And giggled. 'Actually, I just remembered you do that weird dad dancing thing. That won't impress her. Go talk to her instead.'

She made it sound so easy. To a fifteen-year-old, it probably was. He put his arm round her and squished her close. 'Ah, Lily-Bee, I love you so much and I know you're only trying to help, but sometimes…' He sighed. 'Sometimes in life you have to admit defeat.' How many times did he need to admit his feelings to Briana and keep getting the same answer back? She didn't want him. She didn't want him. She didn't want him.

'Nothing I can do or say is going to change her mind and I wouldn't want to back her into a corner. That's not the kind of relationship I want. She has to *want* to be with me. She's an independent woman who makes her own choices and decisions. I have to honour them whether I like them or not. But, for the record, I don't like it. Not at all.'

And now he had to watch from the sidelines. He caught sight of her bump again as she twirled round, now on the dance floor, and his heart just about shattered all over again.

Whatever happened, he'd be fully involved in their child's life. He'd managed it with Lily and he'd manage it again. He'd be there for the first teeth, the first words, the first steps, only not in the way he'd hoped he could be. And perhaps he'd learn to quietly love Briana from a distance. Instead of this burning love close up.

'I think I'll head off. Are you okay to come home with Beth and Alex?'

'Of course.' Lily squeezed his arm. 'I wish I could make things better for you, Dad.'

He smiled. At least this part of his life was improving day by day. 'By saying that, Lily-Bee, you just made everything a whole lot better.'

Briana's heart sank as she looked over to where Fraser had been standing. He wasn't there any more. She scanned the dance floor. He wasn't there either. Or at the bar.

Maybe the toilet?

She watched as different people entered and exited. No. He'd disappeared.

He'd gone.

It's okay.

It wasn't okay. She wasn't okay. Her mouth hurt from the fake smile she'd worn all day. Her heart hurt.

She missed him. There hadn't been a moment since that day in the car park when she'd been relieved about putting a stop to things. She'd been trying to convince herself it was for the best, but her best since then had been the absolutely bloody awful worst.

Working with him was torture. That tiny little clinic area meant they had to negotiate their space and she'd barricaded him out with excuses. But she still breathed him in. Still ached for him. It physically hurt to see him. An awkward tension hung between them.

She'd thought she'd try to break the ice tonight. Somehow. Just try to be a friend at least. But she'd missed her chance. He'd gone. And it would never be the same anyway, not when she wanted to be with him.

She hurt all over again.

'Hey.' Lily came over and gave her a hug.

With a lump in her throat Briana wrapped her arms round her beautiful goddaughter. At least she had this gift in her life. 'You look lovely, Lily.'

'Thanks. So do you.' Lily smiled as she sat down at one of the huge round tables awash with crocheted wedding favours that Rose and Katy had made. 'That colour's nice on you and your bump is starting to show.'

Briana looked down and flattened the silk over her belly. Panic and wonder mixed inside her. 'Is it?'

'Only when you turn sideways. No one else would probably notice. But they will soon.'

'You okay with that?' Bri sat down next to her, hoping her baby's half-sister would grow to love this child.

A little shrug. 'I think so. Yes.'

'It's early days and a bit fresh for all of us. We've got a few more months to get used to the idea. But…if you ever want to come to a scan or anything let me know. Meet this little one before they're even born. Pretty cool, right?'

'A scan? Baby scan?' She looked horrified and delighted at the same time. 'I've seen them on the TV. You hear their heartbeat and see them, like, fully formed.'

'Yes. But no pressure.' And just to remove any pressure Bri changed the subject. 'That's a nice necklace.'

Lily fingered the little heart pendant at her neck. 'Jerome gave it to me.'

'Oh, the sweetheart. He has excellent taste.' At least one of them was having love-life success. 'Is he coming up again soon?'

'No.' The girl sat up straight. Businesslike. Growing up. 'Actually, we've broken up.'

'Oh, dear.' Fraser must have had a hard time navigating this. 'Are you okay about it?'

Lily nodded. She seemed perfectly fine about a break-up. Unlike Briana. 'It was my idea. I don't have time for anything long distance at the moment. Not with the play and everything.'

A break-up had been Briana's idea too but why? Why, when it made her feel like this? She was exhausted and she knew it wasn't just because of the baby. Grief made her weary. She had no energy, no enthusiasm. She just simply missed him. Her life had been so much better when he'd been in it.

She brought herself back to Lily. 'Ah, yes. The play.' Lily had been given a starring role in the school production. 'It must take up a lot of your time. Good call on the Jerome situation.'

'It was his idea I audition for it.'

'Do you miss him?'

As if you have part of you that's been cut off? Do you dream about him? Ache for him? Ache for what you could have had?

'Not really. It was one of those things that fizzles out. Plenty more fish in the sea.' Lily grinned slyly.

'Oh? Is there someone…?'

Lily looked at her through her long eyelashes and tapped her nose. *It's a secret.* 'Early days.'

This was good. Lily was sharing things about her life. 'Well, I'm here if you ever want a chat about anything.'

'Yeah. Thanks.' Lily frowned. 'Actually, my dad…'

Uh-oh. Truth time. Briana sat forward. 'Look, I don't know if he's told you…whatever we had… it's ended. But I'd really like for us all to work together when the baby comes.'

'Do you love him?'

'What?' Briana blinked. Maybe her relationship with Lily needed a few more boundaries.

Or maybe she should be proud Lily was a forthright and confident woman.

'Do you love my dad?' Lily repeated.

'I don't know.'

With all my heart, all my breath, with everything I have.

Bri felt her lip wobble. She couldn't lie to Lily and she couldn't lie to herself any more. 'Yes. Yes, I do.'

'Have you told him?'

'No.' That was met with an eye-roll that reminded Briana that she was opening her heart to a fifteen-year-old. 'It's not as simple as—'

'Right. I'm too young to understand. Okay.' Lily held her palms up. 'I know you love him and I'm pretty sure he loves you. I know he's miserable. And I'm pretty sure you are too. I know he isn't eating properly, and his face looks like the sun has gone in or something. He's told me he's going to be grumpy for the rest of his life. And that's just sad.'

Bri smiled. 'I hope he isn't. That would be terrible.'

'Especially for me.' Her goddaughter grinned. 'Look, I know it's a big thing that you weren't expecting. But you have to take a chance. Take a risk.'

'Wow, Lily.' Briana laughed. 'I don't know what to say.'

Lily leaned in and whispered, 'What would Ellen say?'

Bri gasped at the sharp sting in her chest. Beautiful Ellen, whose life was cruelly taken before it had really started. Ellen, who had told her over and over that Fraser was a good man. That he was a wonderful father. But, of course, Briana knew that and more. He was generous and funny and he hadn't pressured her into anything. In fact, he'd done exactly as she'd asked him to do and left her alone. She couldn't have asked for more.

And she loved him.

She knew what her best friend would encourage her to do, and now her best friend's daughter was saying it too. Two generations couldn't be wrong, surely? She cupped her goddaughter's chin. 'You're a chip off the old block, Lily Moore. You're pure Ellen.'

'And Fraser too.'

'And Fraser too.' His gentleness. His enthusiasm. His open honesty that was at once raw and yet freeing. He believed in her and made her believe it too. He hadn't been afraid to tell her what he wanted, and he'd taken a leap of faith regardless of the consequences. That kind of a man came along once in a lifetime. 'Ellen would say, *Hell, yes*. Go for it.'

'So, does it take a fifteen-year-old to bash your heads together? Talk to him. Talk to each other.'

'And say what?'

'Well, someone wise once told me that what makes you happy is being able to be truly honest with someone. Maybe you could start with that?'

Touché. 'But he's gone.'

'Actually, no. He's standing right there.' Lily pointed out of the French doors behind Briana to a private jetty that led down to the lake. He was alone, his back to her, silhouetted by fairy lights threaded through thick coils of rope fencing and a silvery full moon. In his suit he looked dangerous and magnificent, and the sight of him made her heart dance. Falling in love had been unexpected, unwanted. She'd come home with no plan, looking to hide away from her feelings and experiences and try to make something new for herself.

But it was Fraser who had made her see everything in a new light; he'd helped create this new life inside her. He made her feel renewed and being in his arms made everything feel complete.

Could it be possible that maybe, just maybe, Fraser was her fresh start?

Fraser looked out across the lake breathing in the cool air that blew in from the mountains. In the distance he could hear music, laughter, chatter from the wedding party in the hotel.

He felt detached from it all. Untethered. Adrift.

It was cold, but he didn't care. The breeze reminded him he was alive, and he could breathe out here when he couldn't breathe watching Briana. Every glimpse of her made his chest constrict.

Boy, he had it bad.

'Fraser?'

He whirled round at the sound of her voice, his heart lifting and hurting at the same time. Her bun had come lose and curls hung round her cheeks. She was breathless, her cheeks flushed. She was beautiful. Perfect.

All he wanted to do was take her into his arms and kiss her until his thoughts blurred. But he just nodded, forcing himself to get used to being around her in this faux emotionless state—when in reality the emotion was just shoved down, pushed back, still bubbling under the surface. 'Hey, Bri. You okay?'

'Tired.' She gave a little shrug. 'But okay.'

Why was she here when she'd spent the last few weeks keeping her distance? His eyes dipped to her stomach and his own gut tightened in concern. 'Baby okay?'

'Yes. All is fine.' She suddenly looked nervous and pale. 'Look, Fraser…we need to talk.'

'Did Lily put you up to this?' He mimicked Lily's voice. *'"Go talk to my dad. He's a sad sack who needs cheering up."'*

Bri smiled softly. 'We chatted, yes.'

Ah. Then that explained it. A pity-party. *Great.* 'Take no notice. She's trying to help but probably making it worse.'

'Actually, she helped me clarify a few things.'

'How?' His chest tightened as he waited for more rejection.

'She asked me if I loved you.'

'Oh, God.' He wanted to shrivel up and die right there. 'Sorry.'

'No. No, it's good.' Bri held her palm up. 'She's amazing, Fraser, really. She's a beautiful, young woman and I'm so proud of her. She's not scared of emotions. She doesn't hide from them, she feels them keenly. Lets them work through her system. It's a good thing. And she's not scared to take risks.'

'Don't I know it.' He shook his head. Okay, so she'd come to talk about Lily. The little flicker of hope fizzled out. 'And?'

'And what?'

'The answer to her question.'

She took hold of his hand and looked up at him. Vulnerability and something else…fear, perhaps, or panic…flitted across her gaze. Then determination. Clarity. 'I told her that, yes, I do. I do love you.'

'The way I loved Ellen, right? Friends. Coparents. That's…' He took his hand away from hers. 'Okay.'

He'd get used to it.

'Not like Ellen.' She stepped closer and took his hand again. 'Thing is…you were right. I am scared about making a commitment to you. I'm scared about planning a future with anyone. I told myself you didn't love me, couldn't love me, and I didn't want to hear it when you tried to say those precious words. I hid behind you planning to go back to London. Then when you decided to stay I had nothing to hide behind. I panicked. I'm scared about the way I feel because it's out of control. It's unpredictable. It's wild.'

She laughed. 'It's wonderful. I'm dizzy with it. Lost in it. Lost in you. And that's okay.' She breathed in and nodded, repeating slowly, 'That's okay. I was trying to hold tight onto who I am, who I wanted to be. But I realise now that being with you makes me feel stronger. Braver. More. So much more. You make me believe in myself more than I ever did before. You listen. You hear me. And I know *we* can work it out. I know we'll be a team. Together.'

He couldn't believe she was saying these things. Expecting that any minute there would be a 'but'.

She shook her head. 'I love you, Fraser. Like a friend, like a co-parent, yes. But I'm *in love* with you too. I didn't want to be, I fought against it. I raged against it. I didn't want to be trapped and I know you didn't want anything from me. You definitely didn't want a baby.'

'I do now.' His heart was racing. 'There's going to be more bumps on the road, I'm sure.'

'Then we'll face them together. Ever since that day in the car park I've felt as if a part of me was missing and I…' She took his hand and placed it over her belly. '*We* don't want to live another day without you.'

He blinked, still unable to compute. Had he fallen and hit his head? Was he back in his bed and dreaming? 'Are you saying…?'

'I love you. I want to be with you. I want…' she pointed to her chest and then his '…this.'

'I thought I'd lost you. You didn't want—' His throat was too tight with emotion. His words stuck. He couldn't speak.

'Oh, God.' Her hand went to her mouth. 'Oh, no. I've read it wrong. You've changed your mind. You don't want it.'

'Don't want it?' In a panic he found the words pretty damned quick. If this was a dream he was not going to let it end. He laughed and pulled her close in case she totally got the wrong impression. 'I want you more than anything in the world, Briana Barclay. I want us. I want our family. I want…everything. A new start for all of us. I love you.'

'I love you too.' She slipped into his arms, her face bright with tears and smiles.

And then she kissed him.

EPILOGUE

Six months later...

'BE CAREFUL! WATCH IT! Whoa! Not there! There. Careful. Precious cargo.' Lily hovered around Fraser, shouting directions as he placed the baby car seat onto the bed.

Bri followed them in and sat down in the rocking chair, watching as father and daughter fussed. They seemed to be in a competition about who loved the baby the most.

She reckoned she won. She loved them all so much.

The bedroom was exactly how she'd envisaged it: the cot, the rocking chair, stacks of teeny baby clothes, even though they had a perfectly suitable nursery down the corridor. But she wanted to be on hand when the baby woke up, at least for the first few months. Her new husband agreed.

He grinned. 'I've got it, thanks, Lily.'

'Got *her*.' A Lily eye-roll, which took today's

count to about number one hundred and thirty-four. 'I don't want you to drop her.'

Fraser laughed. 'I meant I'm in control of the car-seat manoeuvre. I've done this a few times.'

'But you haven't done it with this little one.' Lily unclipped the straps on the car seat and carefully picked up little Ellen Josephine Moore— Elle for short—who was making little gurgling sounds, and cradled her in her arms. 'I think she's hungry. Or does she need changing? How do we tell what her different cries mean? Can I change her?'

Bri smiled. It had been an intense labour and she was tired and wired. Excited and hopeful and teary. 'I think we'll learn as we go. Right now, I'd say she's just showing us how excited she is to be home. Just like I am.'

'This is where the fun starts.' Fraser took the squeaking little bundle from Lily and lifted her onto his shoulder, rocked from side to side, patting the tiny back and whispering, 'Hey, there, little Elle-Belle. This is our bedroom. This is your sister, Lily-Bee. She hates the Bee bit, but we say it to wind her up.'

'It works.' Lily snorted and stroked the baby's head, cooing soft words and giving her gentle kisses. 'Don't tell them, but I like it, really.'

'This is your mummy.' Fraser turned and bent to Briana, taking little Elle's hand and waving. He stopped, his beautiful smile turning to a look of concern. 'Oh. God, are you okay? You're crying.'

Briana sniffed and wiped her tears away. 'I'm absolutely fine. Absolutely, wonderfully, totally fine.'

He knelt down next to her and pressed his cheek to hers, protecting the baby on his chest. 'So why the tears?'

'It's so perfect.' She took them all in, her husband and her two beautiful daughters, unable to believe she could be this lucky. This *loved*. Unable to measure the love in her heart, because it was beyond anything she could ever have imagined.

The giving and taking, the wholeness, the care. The unity of it all. 'All of it. All of you. It's just perfect.'

* * * * *